The Fool
and the
Dancing Bear

The Fool
and the
Dancing Bear

by Pamela Stearns

Illustrated by Ann Strugnell

An Atlantic Monthly Press Book

BOSTON   Little, Brown and Company   TORONTO

FIRST EDITION

Library of Congress Cataloging in Publication Data

Stearns, Pamela.
  The fool and the dancing bear.

  "An Atlantic Monthly Press book."
  SUMMARY: A lovesick king, his court jester,
and a bear embark on a quest to lift the curse of
a spiteful queen.
  [1. Fantasy] I. Strugnell, Ann. II. Title.
PZ7.S8124Fo   [Fic]   78-26965
ISBN 0-316-81171-8

ATLANTIC-LITTLE, BROWN BOOKS
ARE PUBLISHED BY
LITTLE, BROWN AND COMPANY
IN ASSOCIATION WITH
THE ATLANTIC MONTHLY PRESS

VB
*Published simultaneously in Canada
by Little, Brown & Company (Canada) Limited*

PRINTED IN THE UNITED STATES OF AMERICA

To B. B.

The Fool
and the
Dancing Bear

Prologue

The guard at the castle gate blocked the stranger's path. "What name?" he demanded. "Are you expected?"

"I have the King's standing invitation," the Jester said. "Say Timon — from Prince Hestle's court. He will know."

A servant went with the message and the guard gestured for Timon to make way for a man carrying a string of partridges and, after him, a man with a basket full of wine bottles slung across his back.

"Some festive affair?" Timon asked eagerly.

"A reception for Queen Alys of Zircon."

"Aargh!" Timon blurted. Beautiful, willful, arrogant, foul-tempered, and notorious for casting spells as carelessly as snow fell — this was Queen Alys of Zircon. Timon caught up his small bundle. "How foolish of me!" he said hastily. "I have suddenly remembered a previous appointment. I must be — somewhere else! Give the King my excuses and —"

But too late.

Rolf, King of Holm, bounded toward him. "At last!" he cried. "We have been waiting! I have boasted to my entire court what a clever fellow you are."

Such words could only please, but Timon drew back from the

3

King's welcome. "There is a man I promised to meet, Your Majesty — at the inn. Let me put him off and then I return."

The King burst into laughter. "We would never see you again, rascal! — and who can blame you? But this wretched Queen will be here only a few hours. You must sit by me and make the time bearable, for we are preparing a reception so dull she will never wish to return."

"But, King," Timon said, "that describes half the receptions that are given. She will scarcely notice."

King Rolf laughed again. "You will see, Sir Impudent — this will be worse than all others."

Timon considered. A few hours — what could happen?

"Since you insist," he said.

But Queen Alys's stay was not boring. The King could arrange an insipid reception but he could not make his own handsome face and form insipid. The Queen no sooner saw him but she loved him and offered her kingdom if he would love and marry her.

While she was falling in love with the King, however, he was falling in love with her sister, Princess Jessy, who stepped next out of the coach, and his love was immediately returned.

Panic raced through Timon's breast as he watched. He had seen the workings of romantic nonsense before. Nothing could come of this but evil.

"Glorious!" a familiar voice purred at his shoulder. "Glorious!" Timon shuddered. Vos! Think *evil* and here was Vos! All in black as always. So appropriate. The man who knew how to screw profits out of stones. Timon had performed several times before the Queen's pale and sleek Minister and knew, to his embarrassment, that Vos thought him very entertaining. "And I expected a dull time!" Vos continued. "What do you think, Fool? — will all this romance end in a banishment? A beheading? Blighted lives? Or maybe a curse? The Queen is superb with curses, you know."

The Queen's large entourage and the King's people sat to a table of tepid dishes, but Timon did not notice. He could not chew or swallow. He could only watch with foreboding the tender and passionate looks that passed between the King and Princess Jessy, and the violent glances the Queen shot at both. Only his promise to the King — how rashly given! — prevented his fleeing from the castle. From the kingdom.

Suddenly the Queen leapt to her feet. "Will you love me, King?" she demanded.

"I cannot, Queen Alys," the King replied with earnest. "I —"

"Enough!" the Queen snapped. She raised her arms toward the ceiling, and as she did so Vos's shrill laugh rang out like the cry of a raven.

Until he loves me, the Queen incanted in a dreadful voice,
Listless be.
Trees and birds and every being,
Fall to dust,
Sprawl to rust,
Minds decline and bodies too.
Until he loves me, cursèd be.
Delight in nothing.
Indolence rule.

She swept from the Great Hall, ordering her men to drag along her sister, who was clinging to the King's hand and weeping.

Vos wrenched their hands apart and, as he propelled her before him, leaned toward Timon with a sneer. "As I said — superb with curses!"

Some time later the King, still stunned, found a note in his hand, which read:

> *Sweetest and bravest of handsome Kings — the*
> *Dancing Bear will come. April Flower knows.*
> *Only the Dancing Bear may lift the curse.*
> *The Queen loves him and will try to kill him.*
>
> *Your Princess.*

Chapter One

The Queen's curse was fast and thorough. In three years the beautiful kingdom was unrecognizable.

The houses were ramshackle. Weeds choked the gardens. Trees were stunted and bare. Potholes and rocks embellished the roads but went unnoticed because there was no wagon or carriage fit to roll. Rain clouds sped across the sky, leaving only enough water to mock paltry kitchen gardens and fields of spiky grain.

The people sprawled indoors yawning and dozing. The only business that functioned was the inn at the edge of the castle town. None went there but the Queen's soldiers, who passed through now that the Queen had annexed Holm, and the occasional stranger who wandered into the kingdom and needed refreshment before hurrying away as fast as his horse could carry him.

Perched on a rock ledge above the town was the castle. Dusty. Dilapidated. Dismal.

The King's friends stayed away, fearing the curse might be contagious. Had they come, it was doubtful the King could have found the energy to entertain them. He only slouched on his threadbare throne, faithfully waiting for the events of the Princess's note to occur, and dreaming of the past. Festivals and fairs. Sumptuous feasts. Balls of incomparable elegance. A beautiful Princess.

"Tell me about the Princess," he said to the Jester, who sat on the floor waiting for the King to make his move on the backgammon board.

"Sire," Timon said, "you have heard it a thousand times. Let me tell you something different. Combat with fearsome monsters, voyages across raging seas, searches for great treasure."

The King shook his head. "The story about the Princess."

Timon sighed and pulled himself to his feet. He did not even remember what the Princess looked like. He remembered little of that day except the din of the curse. But he moved across the dusty floor with waving arms and graceful steps, making up yet another story about handsome King Rolf and beautiful Princess Jessy, who fell in love the instant they saw each other. He sang of separation and hardship and much longing, and finally the story ended — as they all did — with a description of the joyful reuniting and living blissfully into eternity.

Always different but always the same; it was the King's pleasure. One of his few, for the curse had robbed him of everything but his devotion to the Princess.

As Timon paused to catch his breath there was a soft, indecorous snore and he found the King asleep with a smile upon his lips. The sight depressed Timon immeasurably. The King had been a man of quick wit and intelligence. How swift and far had been his fall! And Timon knew his own fate was the same.

He knew he fell more slowly to the curse because he had never had the King's easy life. The agility of his mind and body was like a tough kernel at his center. He lived by it.

And yet he would come to the same end. Every day Timon felt the indolence close about him.

He looked listlessly around the Great Hall, wandered down a corridor, and eventually found himself on the parapet, his eyes sweeping across the torpid valley. Nothing but a small column of soldiers crossing through, uninterested in the castle above. Timon did not care about them.

He was looking for the Dancing Bear.

Nothing could be more absurd. Over and over again he had said to the King, "You cannot be so foolish as to believe this note, sire. For fifteen years bears have been killed on sight in the Queen's lands. What dancing bear will come here?"

Nothing could be more foolish than to stand watching for a bear to come trundling along one of the rutted roads to deliver them. The country was — he laughed bitterly — bare of bears.

Yet he looked for just that bear. And had done it many times. So tenacious was hope.

The laugh died on his lips as he stared at a roll of dust rising from the road. A man appeared to be walking very fast toward the castle. Timon blinked. No man had walked fast in years.

And yet it was nothing else. The man came through the outer gate puffing and gasping so loudly that even the guards were roused.

By the time the fellow stumbled into the Great Hall Timon was perched beside the King, whom he had shaken awake. The three Chamberlains had come, and several courtiers stirred by the commotion.

"The bear — the Dancing Bear —," the man stammered. "At the Inn — the Dancing Bear —"

The words reverberated through the chamber and bounced off the walls.

Stunned gasps filled the room.

"The Dancing Bear!"

"The Dancing Bear!"

Timon turned to the King. His face was contorted and a harassed look clouded his eyes as his indolent brain tried to cope with the news.

"I will bring the bear," Timon said. "It cannot be *the* Dancing Bear —" He looked at the man who had brought the news. "Why do you say he is the Dancing Bear? Did he tell you? Did he dance?"

The man stared blankly and finally stammered, "No — no, sir. He — but he is a *bear!*"

"I thought so," Timon said. "But we must talk to him anyway. He may know something."

"Here?" the King whispered. "You cannot bring him *here.* Vos will find him. The penalty is death for anyone who harbors a bear."

"Vos will not come," Timon said. He had already calculated that Vos would not come for at least two weeks to ask the Queen's perpetual question, "Does the King love me?" and to harass the King by taunting him with rumors of the Princess's imminent betrothal. Vos was jealous of the King. He wanted the Princess for himself, and found King Rolf too handsome, even as he was now.

He would also command a performance from Timon, making the castle ring with his vile laugh and leaving them all feeling they had somehow been soiled.

"You cannot be sure," the King said.

"We must take the chance," Timon said, "before the bear is found by soldiers or some citizen bestirs himself enough to inform for the reward. I will bring him." He looked at the townsman. "At the Inn?"

"Sitting in the corner — drinking ale. A great brown thing with big teeth."

"Charming," Timon murmured.

Chapter Two

Some time later Timon elbowed through the small group huddled outside the door of the Inn and entered the warm gloom
of the place. His nose twitched as the stale smells of ale and dust
and bad food engulfed him. He squinted into the dimness. The
place was deserted except for the hulk at the far corner.

A great brown hulk whose face was partly hidden by a tilted
mug of ale. Bright eyes stared straight into his. The mug came
down and the Bear drew back his lips. Timon's eyebrows went
up. The teeth looked as big as building stones and light glanced
off them as it glanced off shining, sharpened blades.

Since no one was serving, Timon got himself some ale and
leaned on the counter to appraise the situation.

The Bear continued to stare at him with his teeth showing. A
menacing expression — no mistaking that — but since Timon
had not come all this way merely to gawk, he screwed up his
nerve and said in a voice that came out very loud, "I see you
smiling, sir — and I bid you welcome. Let me give you more."

The Bear looked surprised.

"You take this for a smile, Fool?"

"Why, certainly!" Timon piped. "And I am glad to see such
geniality in one who might easily choose to be — how shall I say?

Surly? Unsocial? It bespeaks a generous and openhearted nature, which I am always pleased to come upon."

The Bear grunted and shoved his mug toward Timon.

"You are not reticent," he said.

Timon smiled. After all, he had not been devoured yet. "It is my trade, sir. What is a Fool if not a talking box?" He put the refilled cup near the Bear, who grunted again and muttered inaudible syllables, which Timon chose to interpret as thanks.

"May I sit?" he asked. "I would like to talk with you."

"I would prefer you didn't," the Bear said in civil but firm tones.

Timon was silenced for the moment.

He wiped his hand across his mouth and sat some distance from the Bear, who stared in the direction of a window so dirty it was opaque. From all appearance he no longer remembered Timon.

But jesters did not survive by timidity.

"You are hungry," Timon said baldly. "Let me bring you a meal. Something spicy and succulent. I am myself a gourmet and a cook of no mean talent." This was far from true but it was clear that desperate measures were in order. "My skill is wasted among these people, who would as soon eat boiled shoetops as fine capon stuffed with oysters and wild rice." He touched his hands to the bright cloth around his waist. "I have in this sash many small pockets and in these small pockets, powders of various kinds which have proved useful. Herbs, spices, medicinals. Have you a need? Merely ask and I provide. Things to turn the blandest fare into feasts. Now I ask you, as one who has obviously seen the world and savored its —"

"Enough, Fool," the Bear interrupted, an ominous grate to his voice. "Go talk off the ear of your King or any other poor soul but me."

He turned slightly, giving Timon his massive shoulder, an immovable barrier to conversation.

Timon stared at the mass of fur. This was not the bear they had waited for. Great heavy thing — *he* could be no dancer. Even supposing there was some thin truth to the Princess's note, there could be no connection between Queen Alys and this bear with ale on his lip. Besides, was there any reason *he* should risk bodily harm to get this unsociable creature to the castle? Why had he volunteered to come in the first place? Even idiots knew the folly of *volunteering*.

The answer was simple.

No one else was fit to come.

He thought this without egotism. Before long the curse would make him unfit too. He pressed his palms against his eyes and gave a small moan.

The Bear glanced at him and then away.

Timon pulled himself up.

"They have been waiting for you three years," he said defiantly, "to lift the curse from this kingdom." He took a draft and plunked the cup on the table.

There was a long silence, broken only by insects in the hot grass.

"I am here by mistake," the Bear said in a dispassionate way, not looking at Timon. "Misdirected by some fool. No one waits for me here and I have nothing to do with curses."

"Come and tell it to the King."

"No — *you* tell the King. I have a long way to go."

"Where?"

The bear cast him a wry look which said this was none of his business, then he shrugged. "I am going to the Plain of Waving Grass."

"That is not so far away."

"I am told it is."

Timon did not argue. Considering the dangers that lay between Holm and the Plain of Waving Grass, it might indeed be far away — for a bear.

"The castle is near. You can be away by midafternoon."

"I can be away in two minutes," the Bear said. He drained his cup and stood up. He made for the door, carrying a small portmanteau.

As Timon watched, his breath quickened and his heart thumped against his ribs.

"You are a dancer!" he blurted.

The Bear turned around, pleased.

"You can tell?"

"Who could not?" Timon said. "Every move cries it."

The Bear laughed slightly, a rumble deep in his throat.

"I am retired," he said, "but we never lose it — if I say so myself. I learned it all from a traveling fiddler of rare talent. The nearest thing to a father I ever had. Who but a father would complain so little at having his feet trod upon so often? But I finally outgrew that clumsiness and became quite good — I admit it."

He looked across the room at Timon with something like friendliness.

"I am not the bear you seek. Though even if I were, I confide I would very likely never admit it because this is a miserable and strange place. I will be glad to put it behind me. Even the ale is peculiarly flat. If I had not been so thirsty —" He shrugged.

"Listen to me, Bear — ," Timon called.

But the Bear gave him a cautionary look and shook his head. "No more, Fool."

He went out, paying no heed to the gawkers, who fell away to let him pass.

Timon stared after him. The likelihood that this was *the* Dancing Bear was small. Negligible. Infinitesimal. Why not let him go? And yet —

He hurried out and, as he followed, saw with amazement that the dancer — so unmistakably a dancer! — walked with a slight limp. Pushing this surprise aside, he ran ahead of the Bear and stood in his path. He planted his feet solidly though he knew the Bear could swat him aside with the merest flick of his wrist.

"It *is* a miserable and strange place," he said when the Bear stopped and stared at him more in astonishment than anger. "Leave quickly or you will lose your fine lively gait and your mind will fall into a lazy stupor and you will be like the rest of us. It is the curse."

"Fool — do not tell me to leave quickly while blocking my way and babbling nonsense of curses and stupors."

The Bear raised his paw. Timon gulped but stood firm.

"It is no nonsense, dancing bear. This kingdom is under a curse. It was once green and thriving as any place, the people as lively as any. You have no defense against the curse. Your grace will turn clumsy, your bright eyes dull, your quick mind slovenly. Hurry away!"

The Bear stared down at Timon with glinting eyes. "Fools are ever fools," he said. "It is nothing to me that you make up extravagant tales of curses. Only do not bother me with them. Move! I must be on my way!"

Timon leapt and kicked his heels. "Hah!" he barked in a mocking and insulting tone. "I have convinced you and you flee. Wise! Most wise, Bear!" He jumped to the side of the road and swept a low bow. "Hurry, hurry! There is no knowing how swiftly works the curse. You have already been here — how long?" His eyes sought the position of the sun. "Each minute tells! Let me detain you no longer! Farewell, dancing bear! Let all who can flee do so! It will be our secret. You and I know it is not cowards who flee but the wise."

He found himself lifted off the ground and staring straight into bright, infuriated eyes.

"Devious windbag! Think to take me in with such a paltry trick? Think again." The Bear slammed him back to the ground so hard Timon thought he must have gone into the road like a driven stake.

"Think to fool this Fool with brave words while you flee as fast as feet will carry you?" he shouted. "On your way, brave dancing bear! Make no excuses to me. Nothing is clearer than that we await another bear — not you! I only thank the gods that I did not take you to the King. Why, his people would laugh themselves unconscious and I would never hear the end of it."

He turned his back on the Bear and walked away with quaking knees, expecting to be laid out with a blow.

A hairy paw and sharp claws lifted him by the scruff and a dreadful voice growled in his ear, "Where is this King?"

Chapter Three

Timon took one look at the meal that came up from the kitchens and decided that the Bear must be distracted from the food. So instead of taking his place beside the King he put on a performance, this time telling the true story of the Queen's fateful visit and the curse.

The Bear only frowned. He frowned at his plate as if this were the worst meal he had had in days, and he frowned at Timon as if this were the worse act he had seen in his life.

When Timon ended the tale with the part about the Dancing Bear who would lift the curse, the Bear pushed his plate away and said, "You are the cook of great talent, Fool — why didn't you cook for us?"

"Eh?" the King muttered.

Timon laughed. "A bald-faced lie, I fear."

The Bear laughed too. "I thought so. And what of your many powders in their many small pockets that can make a feast of the blandest fare?"

Timon's ears reddened. "The pockets exist and the powders exist — all that is true," he said, "but the friend who gave me the sash did not teach me to use the cooking powders in any refined way." He frowned as the Bear let out a mocking laugh. "But if your head throbs or you cannot sleep —"

"I know," the Bear interrupted. "You will *talk* me to blessed oblivion."

Now, mockery was the Jester's stock in trade and nothing delighted Timon more than serving up a clever jibe, but mockery turned on himself was something else. His fists balled and he glared at the Bear with his jaws clenched. If he opened his mouth he would lose his temper and that was against all his professional standards. Instead, regaining his self-control, he changed the subject. "So — will you help King Rolf?"

The Bear was entirely surprised. "Help him what?"

"You are a dancing bear."

"But even if some particle of your story is true — which I doubt — I am not *the* Dancing Bear."

"Think hard," the King said disconsolately. "Perhaps you have forgotten." He pushed his dishes away, curled his arms on the table and dropped his chin on them.

"I have heard of Queen Alys, of course —," the Bear said. "Who has not? She is famous for her beauty and notorious for her arrogance. And she is infamous for her persecution of bears. Now you tell me a bear is the only one who can influence her to lift your curse. This is rank nonsense."

The King groaned. He turned to the First Chamberlain. "Haven't they found it yet? It can't be *lost!* The very note *itself!* How could it be *misplaced?*" He looked at the Bear. "I put it in a treasure box — so it couldn't wear away from the mere folding and unfolding, you know. Now these — Timon, haven't you seen the box somewhere? What happened to the note after you saw it? You can't have *forgotten!*"

The Jester gave a careless shrug but his look was grim. Every lapse of memory lay like a cold hand on his heart, another sign of the curse creeping upon him. He remembered the treasure box on this very table. He remembered the King himself putting the note into it, closing it, securing the latch. And nothing more.

He pressed his fingers to his forehead and shut his eyes tight, pushing the treasure box from his mind and trying to summon up the exact words of the note. As he racked his brain his lips worked silently and his fingernails made dents in his forehead. So long since there had been any need for accuracy.

Slowly the words formed in his mind and he could see them on a sheet of white paper, written in a clear, rather sweet script:

> *The Dancing Bear will come. April Flower knows.*
> *Only the Dancing Bear may lift the curse. The*
> *Queen loves him* and will try to kill him.

The Jester's eyes flew open and he gaped at the Bear.

He went to the King's side and murmured, "I have remembered what the note said — and I think we would rather it stay misplaced."

King Rolf turned baffled eyes on him. As Timon leaned and whispered the Princess's words into his ear the King gulped and smiled foolishly at the Bear, who watched with bland interest.

"Call off the search," Timon said when the King did nothing. "I have remembered the exact words of the Princess's note." The Bear's brows lifted but he said nothing. "I quote: 'The Dancing Bear will come. April Flower knows. Only the Dancing Bear may lift the curse. The Queen loves him.'"

"Good for the Dancing Bear," the Bear said. Timon saw no suspicion in his eyes. "But this has nothing to do with me. I'll be going. I thank you for the meal — such as it was."

As he rose Timon gave the King a hard nudge and whispered out of the side of his mouth, "He mustn't go!"

The King nodded and motioned to his guards, who moved not very quickly to block the doorway with raised spears. Timon groaned and threw up his hands. The Bear cast the King a look of mild incredulity and gave his rumble of a laugh.

"You're joking," he said.

Timon rushed forward with a strained laugh. He yanked the weapons from the guards' hands and threw them clattering to the floor. "Hah hah! Certainly the King is joking. Merely a test of the men's alertness. How stale they do get in this peaceful kingdom. Now, Bear, if —"

"Don't talk to me, Fool. You got me here with your blathering tongue — your tongue and my bad temper. I've talked to your King, now I'm going. Get these men out of my way."

The guards scrambled aside without a word of instruction as the Bear strode toward them.

Timon ran to the King.

"Talk to him, King — plead with him. No one else will lift this curse and bring us back to life."

"But he says he is not the one."

"What other one do we have? Maybe he will do. We must find out."

"He'll make pulp of the men if they try to stop him."

"*Now* you think of that!" the Jester cried. "*Bribe* him! Offer the Royal Jewels. They must be —"

King Rolf drew himself up surprisingly. "Offer the Royal Jewels? The Royal Jewels? Now you've gone too far, Fool! Quite out —"

They didn't notice that the Bear had come back from the door. So when he spoke, right at the King's elbow, they both jumped.

"Offer the Royal Jewels," he said. "I may consider."

"What is there for you to consider?" the King said accusingly. "You say you are not the one."

"Listen to your Fool. What other bear do you have? I may do. Let me see the jewels."

The King stood up and covered his ears with his hands. "This is too much! The Royal Jewels! Never! Even if we knew where they were! I'm getting very tired."

He beckoned and two servants helped him upstairs.

As they disappeared around the curve of the steps the Bear said, "What is this about the jewels being lost? They are no good to me lost. This is an incredibly ramshackle place."

"You surprise me," Timon said slightingly. "Bribery was a suggestion made in desperation. I would not have thought you could be diverted by mere jewels. What about the Plain of Waving Grass?"

The Bear gave him a long, unfathomable look, then shrugged. "I will get there." He walked away and said without looking back, "You are sure the jewels exist?"

"Of course they exist. This is a Royal House."

The Bear glanced around the shabby Great Hall. "Who would guess it?"

The jewels were found some hours later in a trunk under the King's bed. They were soon spread out on the dining table.

One crown. A chain. Three rings. One scepter. Two fibulae. An orb and a chalice. All the precious metal — even the gold —

woefully tarnished, but not the stones. Diamonds, rubies, emeralds, sapphires, amethysts — shining, winking, flashing, glimmering, glittering, flickering — like the starry night of some incredible dream.

Timon could only stare, and the King, who had grumbled and fussed but been overruled by his jester, was speechless. He had long ago forgotten the magnificence of the Royal Jewels.

The Bear gazed at the array and picked up the rings. He turned them in his paw. "It is not enough," he murmured.

Timon's head snapped up and he leapt onto his chair. "Not enough!" he shouted. "Not enough! It's all we *have!* What kind of blackguard —"

The Bear looked at him and blinked in surprise. "What?"

"You said it's not enough! You said —"

"Did I?" He turned to the King. "I'm sorry — I was thinking of something else."

"You mean they will — do?" the King asked.

"Oh yes," the Bear replied. "You consent?"

The King bit his lip and covered his eyes with his hand. "What shall I do?" he muttered. "They are not precisely *mine,* you know — the crown, the scepter — Not mine *personally.* They belong to — the *House.*"

"And much good they are doing the House now," Timon said. "The *House* falls down around your ears. You can have new ones made."

The King was shocked. "*Make new ones?* I never heard of such a thing. Where is your sense of *tradition?*"

"I think it must be dying of a curse," Timon said.

The King's mouth snapped shut but his eyes were fevered.

Timon leaned close to him and said in an undertone, "Perhaps the Bear is not as mercenary as he seems. When it is over we will persuade him to give back the jewels."

"Not a chance," the Bear said.

The King waved both away. He slumped into his chair with his eyes closed and his hands clutching his temples. Finally he looked up. "If it must be! Take them, Bear. Take the — the *shining lights* of my House." With a groan of regret and fatigue he beckoned to his servants and almost fell asleep before they reached him.

The Bear slipped the jewels into his portmanteau and clamped his great paw upon it.

"Now, Fool — what do you want of me?"

Chapter Four

The temperature plummeted as the light went. Dank cold settled into the walls, and drafts shot through the corridors and chambers of King Rolf's porous castle. The Jester and the Bear sat considering before a weak fire.

Timon stuck a dry cracker into his mouth.

"It is not a matter of simply presenting ourselves to Queen Alys," he said, "and announcing 'Here is the Dancing Bear — lift the curse!' Especially when we know you are not the right bear. She is —"

"Bound to notice," the Bear said drily.

Timon's eyebrows shot up. Exactly what *he* was going to say! He gave a snort. "And yet even that is uncertain," he said. "I do not have the faith in this note that the King has. It may be utter nonsense — or inaccurate.

"The Queen's father had a dancing bear, much loved by the Queen — Princess then. He deserted the court to join an itinerant theatrical troupe and she has never forgiven him." He waved a hand carelessly. "So she orders all bears killed. We have supposed this is the bear the note speaks of —"

"The bear that she *loves?*"

Timon nodded eagerly. "Unlikely! — to say the least. That's why I say the Princess may have been inaccurate. Perhaps instead

of *the* Dancing Bear, she should have written *a* Dancing Bear —
in which case you might do very well."

"Then we must ask the Princess herself," the Bear said from
the depths of his tall-backed chair.

Even before he finished Timon shook his head. "We tried that,"
he said. "We rode after her as soon as we could. We tried to get
into the castle by hanging onto the undersides of farm wagons,
but they all are searched.

"We tried to row across the lake at night, but torches and
lanterns were everywhere and our boat was sunk by the cata-
pults. The Queen warned King Rolf to forget the Princess and
had us escorted back here. She taunted us for believing the note
and —"

The Bear looked up sharply. "How did she know about that?
Wagging tongues in her party — or here?"

"She got it out of the Princess herself."

The Bear grunted disdainfully. "How unromantic of her. The
King must have been crushed."

"Not so," Timon said. "We were told she talked because the
Queen threatened someone else."

The Bear gave a slight nod. "So you did not see the Princess at
all?"

Timon shrugged. "The King fancied he saw her watching our
unceremonious departure from a high window. He says she stood
in an aura of light and beauty."

"Very helpful," the Bear said. "Light and beauty, is it? Moonstruck ninny! He could be dangerous."

Timon cast him a look of anger, never mind that he had called
the King moonstruck himself. "He was not called the Shining

27

King for nothing," he said. "It is not his fault that the curse has crept all through his bones so that he can do nothing but dwell on his love."

There was no reply and the next thing Timon knew the Bear was saying gently, "Wake up, Fool — we have plans to make."

Timon opened his eyes and blinked and realized he had fallen asleep. More sign of the curse. A cold fear seized him and passed.

He stared at the red embers of the dying fire. The Bear threw on more wood. "If not the Princess, we must find this April Flower," he said. "It is a person, I suppose. Not some — plant."

"April Flower is a clairvoyant."

The Bear looked up slowly. "A clairvoyant?" he said. "One who claims to know what others do not, and who will drag a stranger off the street to mutter nonsensical instructions to him?"

The corner of Timon's mouth twitched. "So you have experience with them."

"But they got no money from me," the Bear said with satisfaction. "Is this what we are to deal with? — marketplace charlatans?"

Now Timon did laugh. "You are brave, Bear. Many credit clairvoyants with all manner of sorcery and magic and are afraid of them. Yours may have been charlatans, but April Flower is no minor practitioner. She was the Queen's clairvoyant and the Queen's father's before that, until there was a quarrel over the Princess and April Flower was banished. She is rumored to live now in the Green Hills. We were not able to find her before —" He shrugged. He was weary of talk of the curse.

The Bear nodded comprehension. "Then we must find her," he said crisply. "In the morning we start for the Green Hills. A strong mount for me, one for you, and a pack horse. I suppose your kitchens —"

"What about the King?" Timon interrupted in a bristling tone. Who, after all, had appointed this bear master of the undertaking?

The Bear looked at him with surprise. "What about him? He stays here."

"The King goes or no one goes," Timon said.

"He will slow us to turtle's pace."

"Then we go at turtle's pace."

The Bear's anger blazed out of his eyes. "What can he do that we cannot?" he asked in a still voice.

"Nothing. But I will not leave him here. If you want the jewels the King must go."

The Bear stared at him and seemed about to make some disparaging remark, then said only, "We will see what he says. Ask him now."

"*Now?* An avalanche and an earthquake will not wake him."

"Then perhaps a bear can," the Bear said. "There are plans to be made and they cannot wait upon this king's — hibernation."

He rose and made for the stairway, obviously ready to waken the King by rattling his bed to kindling, if not by holding him upside down and rattling *him.* Timon shot ahead, saying, "I'll do it."

Finally, after much shaking and shouting, they got the King sitting up three-quarters awake.

Timon had scarcely finished telling the King their plan when the Bear said, "You do not wish to go, do you, King? Such a tedious and dirty trip."

The King looked at him with sleepy dismay. "Certainly I don't wish to go. I hope you didn't wake me to ask *that*."

The Bear shot Timon an arch smile, grasped his arm and began to drag him out of the room.

Timon freed himself with a twist. "Certainly you wish to go, King! Surely you, of all men, will not leave this to others while you idle upon your throne."

The King sat up a little straighter in his rumpled bedclothes. "Of course I must go. I was not thinking — so *sleepy*. You make the plans, Timon, and tomorrow I'll see what I think of them."

"Rutted roads," the Bear said over Timon's shoulder. "Broken wheels, broken shafts, lame horses, scorching sun."

The King looked at him with rising alarm.

"Wind, dust, bad food, strange water, beds stranger still, atrocious —"

"Pay him no heed," Timon interrupted, seeing how the King wavered. "If these things come, they must be borne, sire. You cannot sit back while others lift the curse that was laid because the Queen loves *you*."

The Bear knew by the light that leapt into King Rolf's eyes that he had lost. He stalked from the room and when Timon returned to the fire he found himself the target of a fierce glare.

"I suppose there is some reason you insist upon this — hindrance," the Bear said.

Timon sank back in the chair. "He fades so fast because he does nothing but lie about, and his mind deteriorates into this jelly of romanticism because it has nothing else to consider. This journey may come to nothing but he must make it if only for the — *bracing discomfort*."

The Bear regarded him carefully. "You are fond of this King, Fool?"

Timon's eyes narrowed. "Men of my profession do not become *fond* or *unfond*. Such feelings remove objectivity and turn our tongues either bitter or sweet. Neither will do. But he was quick, intelligent, agile. One does not like to watch the deterioration of such qualities."

Something in the Bear's eyes told Timon he knew he was talking about himself as well as the King. He looked away and the silence hung between them a long moment, then the Bear said, "A small carriage, the carriage driver. Will the King insist on servants and much baggage? The lighter we are the faster we go. Perhaps —"

"Haven't you *grasped* what we've said about the curse?" Timon interrupted. "There are no horses fit to pull a carriage — even supposing there was a carriage fit to go upon a road and a road fit for a carriage to go upon. There is certainly no horse to carry anyone of your size — if such a beast has ever existed.

"Nor can we walk," he continued, talking straight through the interruption the Bear attempted, "because you cannot travel in the open. The Queen's men roam everywhere — here as well as in her own land. They will kill you if they see you."

"Kill me!" the Bear roared.

Timon looked at him with surprise. "You said you know the Queen persecutes bears."

"*Did.*"

"*Does!*" Timon said. "*Does!* You must come from a long way off indeed! Her vendetta against your kind has no end."

The Bear was silent a long time and then said, "I have not

seen a single soldier since I set foot in this wretched place —
except for the King's sorry lot."

"That is your luck."

"But if this is the cursed wasteland you say it is, what interest
do the Queen's men have in it? There cannot still be bears here."

"High in the hills and in the deep forests," the Jester said,
"where soldiers and hunters are afraid to go. The soldiers roam
here to observe for the Queen's Minister. Vos must know everything."

The Bear seemed to retreat into the depths of the chair. When
he spoke his voice dripped sarcasm. "I thank you for not warning
me of these dangers when we first met. What excitement you have
given my life."

Timon's face became expressionless. Would sarcasm be the
Bear's only reaction if he knew just how deceived he was — if he
knew the whole content of the Princess's note? *The Queen loves
him and will try to kill him.*

The Bear took three walnuts in his paw and by making a fist,
cracked them open. As he picked at the meat with deft claws
Timon expected him to say their bargain no longer stood. What
good would Royal Jewels be to him if he were dead? Instead he
only said, "And yet the note says that the Queen loves this Dancing Bear."

Timon stared into the fire. "It is an enigma, is it not?"

They sat without speaking, no sound about them except the
crackle of the fire and the moan of the wind.

Suddenly the shadow of an idea began to form at the back of
Timon's mind. He smiled as it blossomed, and then chuckled. The
Bear looked up.

"It is brilliant," Timon said, "but it will not please you, Bear. Only remember that you have offered no better plan."

"What is it?" the Bear said with a suspicious growl.

Timon told him, and the quiet of the Great Hall was shattered by an outraged "Oh no! Think again, Fool! Not *me!*" which came so loud and terrible from the Bear that the guards bolted upright and stared at each other a full two seconds before falling asleep again. The outcry was followed by Timon's merry chortling, more low talking, and the Bear's aggrieved "Never!"

In the small hours Timon showed the Bear to the bedchamber adjoining his own, then barely managed to drag to his own bed and peel off his clothes before falling unconscious.

He stirred and raised upon his elbows, wakened by soft scraping noises. He blinked and realized slowly that the noise was coming from the next room. The Bear moving furniture — or some other odd thing an odd bear might do. He pulled up the covers and slept.

The sun was high as the party assembled in the castle yard.

A small closed carriage that had once been elegant but was now extensively patched. A chest lashed atop, containing provisions. The King, lodged inside, looking weary and apprehensive. Timon, eager to be off. The Bear in a dress of black mourning borrowed from the largest woman in the town, with shoes on his hind paws and black gloves on his forepaws, and on his head a black hat with a heavy veil thrown back over it.

"But you must put down the veil, Bear," Timon cried, quaking with laughter and staying well out of the galled Bear's reach.

"Fool — I will kill you for this!" the Bear growled. "I will take you in my claws and one by one break every bone in that sorry body."

The King peered out. Their bickering tired him, yet he could not entirely stifle a chuckle at the sight of the Bear.

"I think you will do nicely, Bear," he said. "Without a doubt the finest looking matron in the kingdom." As the Bear whirled on him with his great teeth showing, the King ducked back and pulled the curtain shut.

Timon jumped onto the driver's seat at the front of the carriage. "Be a good sport, Bear. You offered nothing better. Now, shouldn't we be starting?" He motioned toward the shafts.

The Bear growled. He clutched savagely at the voluminous skirts. "*No — not your beast of burden too!*" With that he stalked toward the gates carrying his portmanteau.

"Shall the King walk too?" Timon called. "A slow journey indeed, if the King must walk."

The Bear returned.

He opened the carriage door and thrust in the bag. "I give it to your care, King," he said in a surly tone, "but remember it is mine, and everything in it."

"You think I will steal them back after we have agreed?"

"No, sir — I only wish things clearly understood."

The King huffed and jerked the door shut.

The Bear stood between the shafts, bent slightly toward them then suddenly spun around.

"You!" he shouted at Timon on his perch. "*Off!*"

Timon raised his hands and opened his mouth to protest but the gleam of the black eyes shut him up and he jumped nimbly down.

"I only thought it would distribute the weight more evenly and be of a help to you," he said, dancing a good distance from the Bear.

For reply he got only a look of scorn.

Then with disgruntled mumbling and muttering the Bear picked up the shafts and the carriage rolled through the gates.

The Bear spoke to no one and seemed to hear nothing of the conversation between the King and Timon, who walked alongside the carriage. Occasionally, without warning, he broke into a run and looked back, laughing loudly as Timon huffed and churned to keep up.

They finally stopped beside a sluggish stream, where the Bear set about making camp, not hesitating to direct Timon to do one mean task after another. This grated, and Timon would have protested loudly if only he had known how to do any of these things a better way, or if the Bear had not done the bulk of the work.

After a dinner of leftovers from the previous night they settled on the ground to sleep, the King and Timon with much complaining and the Bear without a word. He lay in the dry grass grasping the portmanteau and staring into the sky.

Next morning they had gone a short way in the dazzling sun when the Bear stopped, appeared to listen for something.

"Riders," he said, then began pulling again.

Soon riders appeared over the crest of the nearby hill.

There were seven, in the green and yellow doublets and black hose of the Queen's mounted soldiers. They paused at the top of the hill then, at a shout from the one with a captain's white plume in his helmet, charged toward the King's carriage with great clattering.

The Bear dropped the shafts and stepped away from them. He pulled a black handkerchief from his pocket, bent his head and dabbed at his eyes and moaned as though he were at that moment standing beside the grave.

The captain reined in beside the carriage and stared from the Bear to the Jester.

"Explain this, Fool," he said brusquely. "Why is this woman in mourning pulling the carriage?" He leaned down and pushed aside the curtain that hid the King.

"King Rolf of Holm, General," Timon said. He was not unnerved by this encounter but pleased that his wits should be tested. He gestured toward the faded crest on the door of the carriage. "The King is ill. We journey to the mineral springs in the Cool Side."

Indeed King Rolf looked unwell, sunk among the old cushions with his lank thin hand cast against his forehead.

The soldier let the curtain fall back.

"You have not answered my question. Why is this woman pulling?"

Timon stepped right up to the soldier. "General, you know there are no horses in this cursed kingdom to pull a carriage. Nor men neither. This substantial lady is my old aunt, in mourning for my uncle dead only these three days. She came because I am her only family now, and no sooner does she arrive than she is pressed into service by the King. We are all subjects, are we not?"

The soldier gave the Bear a long look. The Bear sobbed into the handkerchief. His shoulders shook with uncontrollable grief.

"Leave off, old aunt," Timon said. "This is no way to behave in front of the Queen's General. She is in a bad way and fragile

37

for all her sturdy appearance, sir. Married fifty years to my uncle, with twelve children and now none left but herself. At the end of her tether — who cannot understand and sympathize?" He clicked his tongue and shook his head at the sadness of it all.

"This is a fine King," the soldier said, "who forces a widow to pull him."

"But we have all heard, have we not," Timon said, "of how Vos conscripts women — older and thinner — to do harder work on the Queen's residences?"

The captain gave him a sharp look. "It is not for you to judge the Queen's agent, Fool." Still he stared at the Bear. "Your old aunt, is it? A giant of a woman and you such a pipsqueak."

It was a gross exaggeration and *pipsqueak* rankled. "It runs in our family, General."

"What runs in your family? — shortness or tallness?"

"Why, sir — the extremes," Timon said, and was unable to keep the corners of his mouth still.

"Wretch!" the soldier barked, raising his whip. "Do you think we will stand here to be the butt of your jokes?"

Timon swept him a servile bow, realizing his busy tongue had served him badly. He had made up the story about his aunt to taunt the Bear and now, insisting upon his little joke, he had only succeeded in making the soldier angry. Any man with half a brain would have said nothing, claimed no knowledge of the large woman. But no — the Fool must play the fool.

"Sir," he said in a placating voice, "it is far to the Cool Side, and the King —"

"No, not yet," the soldier said sharply. "You are too glib. There is something —" He jogged the horse toward the Bear. "Old woman, let me see if I know you."

Chapter Five

The Bear's gloved paws tightened around the handkerchief and all his muscles tensed.

Perspiration broke on Timon's forehead. The soldier reached a hand toward the veil and was about to raise it when from the confines of the carriage came a voice dreadful with rage and arrogance.

"Fool! Enough of this! Have we come all this way to sit in the sun and be turned into raisins? Lay the whip to your aunt! Move!"

Timon gulped. "Sire — these soldiers —"

The curtain was whisked aside by a thin hand weighted by three huge rings with jewels that caught the sun and threw it back a hundred times brighter. Their light flashed into the captain's eyes. He raised his hand to cut the glare, and reined the horse to the carriage. The King stuck his head into the sun and glowered at the soldier. On his head was the tarnished but definitely royal crown.

"You mean to impede a King, Lieutenant?" he raged in a fine imperious bellow. "Is that what you mean to do? Brave fellow! Jester — note his name so that we may inform the Queen which of her men was so helpful when we were on our way to take the cure."

The soldier paled.

He gave the Bear and the Jester a quick look, then stiffened and said in a rigid monotone, "Do you wish for escort, sire? The Turmaks have been active across the border."

"No, no — they would not dare," the King said, impatiently thumping the crest on the carriage door.

"Perhaps, sire," the officer said. "But —"

"But nothing! Have we your kind leave to continue, Corporal?"

The officer drew himself up further, and when he spoke his lips scarcely moved. "Certainly, sire." He gave a quick salute, a perfunctory bow. "Good journey," he said and none of the three doubted he would be pleased if the Turmaks stripped them to the skin.

He signaled his men to form into pairs and they rode off, leaving only a column of pale dust.

Timon leaned toward the drawn curtain of the carriage. "Superb, sire!" he whispered loudly, keeping his eyes on the soldiers' retreat. All the answer he got was a gasp and when he opened the door he found the King collapsed against the cushions. His fingers were pressed against his heaving chest and the crown lay at his feet, where it had tumbled.

"Is he all right?" the Bear asked, looking over Timon's shoulder.

Instead of answering Timon pulled out a handkerchief. He poured water into it from the corked jug in the corner of the carriage and held the cloth to the King's forehead.

"Get us out of the sun," he said, for though the inside of the carriage was shaded the air was hot and still.

Without a word the Bear closed the door and in a moment the carriage was bumping along. Soon it stopped and the Bear opened the door. The King was breathing more evenly but seemed barely conscious. Timon poured more water on the handkerchief and left it folded on the King's forehead, then came out to find the carriage in the shadow of a pile of boulders.

The Bear had taken down the food basket and was spreading a few things on a cloth. He looked up. "Will he be all right? What happened?"

Timon nodded and ran his damp hand across his forehead. "It's in him still, you see — the wit to do something like this. But it's getting buried deeper and deeper in the romantic mire. The effort to dredge it up when he must leaves him —" He gestured toward the carriage. He picked up a gherkin and chewed on it. "Of course it's been a long time since he — felt the need to exert himself so. I feared he had lost the power altogether."

They ate in silence for a few minutes, until the Bear said, "Of course this exertion would have been unnecessary if you had held your tongue. Except for King Rolf's brilliance we might have paid a high price for your *jokes*."

Timon's fingers tightened around his wooden cup and he stared in fury. "Do you think you need to tell me?" he snapped. "Though I wonder if the officer would have delayed so long if you had not made him suspicious with your overdone moaning and trembling."

The Bear's eyes glinted. "Oh, no! You will not turn —" He broke off suddenly. He stood up, gave Timon a mocking laugh and walked away. Timon glared at his retreating back.

The Bear returned just as the King stepped shakily out of the carriage and sank into the dry grass.

"An inspiration, King!" the Bear said. "You saved us." He grasped the King's hand.

"Did I?"

"Of course!" Timon said. "It was brilliant."

"Well —," the King said with a broadening smile. "It seemed — it seemed the only thing."

"And it was!" Timon handed the Bear a cup of wine and refilled his own.

The cups were raised in a toast when the Bear suddenly made a silencing motion. "Someone's coming," he said, pulling the veil over his face and darting out of sight behind the rocks.

Timon and the King squinted into the sun and saw a thin figure straggling purposefully toward them from the direction they had come. The man was a stranger to both, but he fell to his knees before the King and thrust a rolled message at him.

"The First Chamberlain's seal!" King Rolf exclaimed. He broke the wax and perused the parchment with a deepening frown.

"*What is it,* King?" Timon asked, barely restraining himself from tearing the message from the King's hands.

But the King ignored him, and when he finally looked up all he said was, "Who are you, sir? How do you have this?"

"A — relay, you might say, Your Majesty," the gasping man replied. "My neighbor brought it to me. And his neighbor to him. I was afraid I would not be able to catch you."

"Some wine for this fine fellow," King Rolf said to Timon, who nearly growled.

Finally, after not one but two cups, the fine fellow left.

"*What,* sire?" Timon blurted, reaching for the paper. It was snatched away by the Bear, who read aloud:

42

*Soon after Your Majesty departed a man
(gap-toothed, green hat) arrived enquiring if a
bear was or had been here. Of course we denied
knowledge of any bear. We were unable to
draw out of him where he got this preposterous
idea. Informed him Your Majesty was heading
for Sanring and saw him head in that direction.
Good journey.*

1st Chmbln

"Who is it?" the Bear asked. "How could he know?"

"A spy," Timon said. "Or a hunter. I warned you, King — someone informed for the reward."

"Then why did one man go to the castle instead of soldiers?" the Bear asked.

"No one informs to soldiers if there is a spy or a hunter about. Soldiers pay nothing until the information is proven. Hunters and spies work alone."

The Bear gave a grim laugh. "Informers, soldiers, spies, hunters — a delightful journey. You will at least tell me that Sanring is in the opposite direction from that we take."

"Of course," the King bristled. "My people are not fools."

"I am glad to hear it," the Bear said drily. Then he smiled. "No insult intended, King Rolf — I am only cautious. We will hope the fellow is overwhelmed by the beauty of Sanring and settles there, or that he commits some petty crime and is jailed."

"Something is strange here," Timon said. "You were at the castle nearly eighteen hours. Why did he take so long to get there?"

The Bear's eyes narrowed. After a moment he said, "Before

this news came I was going to say that we must abandon our charade. Now there is even more reason."

"But it has done splendidly!" the King exclaimed.

"You do not like playing the widow — that's all," Timon protested.

The Bear ignored him. "Until we cross the border we travel by night."

"No!" the King protested. "Of all things I detest most traveling at night! There is no *reason.* Our ruse has done well."

"This far," the Bear said. "But now that the soldiers know who you are, the situation is altered. We had not considered what would be the consequence of the Queen learning you are traveling."

"Ah!" Timon blurted. "I should have thought of that. He is right, King. It is likely word is already going to Queen Alys that you have left your castle and are heading out of Holm. The Queen will be suspicious and will have you questioned — or watched."

"It is not forbidden that I travel," King Rolf said plaintively. "We tell her I am going for the cure — as we told the soldier."

"Then she will send an escort," Timon said. "And do not forget she knows the contents of the note. You suddenly leave your kingdom and travel toward the forbidden Princess and the clairvoyant as well. The Queen is shrewd. Do not underestimate her. It might even occur to her that the substantial widow is not a woman but the Dancing Bear."

"He's right," the Bear said. "Also, no vehicle without an escort will be safe from robbers — who are these Turmaks? Highwaymen?"

The King only groaned.

"An alien and violent tribe," Timon said. "Thieves and plunderers. Obviously they do not come into Holm — there is nothing for them in this desert — but they are rampant in Zircon in spite of the Queen's soldiers."

"More and more delightful!" the Bear murmured. "We will travel at night until we cross into Zircon. I will wear this ridiculous dress as a precaution until we are over the border. Then, if it is true that only your kingdom is under curse and we find live horses across the border, we buy a closed wagon and horses and the King and I ride inside."

"Don't tell me —," Timon said slowly. "Let me *guess* — which of us that leaves to drive."

The Bear's eyes sparkled. "I knew you were perceptive," he said. "And you will dress like a peasant because —"

"Stop! You go too far!" Timon shouted. "My clothes have seen better days but they come by their wounds honorably. I am a jester — this is the raiment of my profession. *I* dress like a peasant? In a flopping coarse shirt and shapeless breeches and great evil-looking boots? Never! Not I! Not if —"

King Rolf clutched at his temples. "Peace, Fool! Let the Bear finish."

Timon glared at the King and barely held back the words that rushed to his lips — *Fine and good for you to listen to the Bear when he says you ride inside!* He bit his lip and walked away.

"Because," the Bear said as coolly as if Timon had never spoken, "we must look ordinary."

"*Ordinary!*" Timon shouted. "I could not look *ordinary* if —"

"But perhaps you are such a good actor that you might manage it," the Bear said.

Timon paused. He considered, shrugged, and said, "For what reason do we adopt all this *ordinariness?*"

"Not merely ordinary," the Bear said, "but definitely on the shabby side."

This drew an aghast "Shabby!" from the King.

"A dark and depressing sight we must present on the road," the Bear continued, "from which passersby will recoil and soldiers manufacture excuses why they should not stop."

Timon looked at the Bear with narrowed eyes, sensing the great sober creature was about to burst his sides laughing.

"What has got hold of your brain, Bear?" he said. "What kind of wagon would soldiers not stop?"

The Bear's eyes fairly danced. He broke off a branch and tied his black handkerchief to one end. Then he walked to the carriage and stuck the stick in the corner of the driver's box. A slight breeze, coming like an omen, caught it and billowed it out like a flag to mark some dread place.

The Bear let out a bark of laughter.

"Who is brave enough to stop the contagion wagon?"

Chapter Six

The King's face turned white. He stared at the Bear as if he had told some foul joke.

Timon was staring at the Bear differently. Suddenly he laughed and threw up his arms.

"Superb! Absolutely superb! Beautiful! *Exquisite!*" he cried. "Bear, I confess I have not appreciated you properly. I would not have guessed you had this in you. It will ever be the regret of my life that I did not think of it myself."

"Timon!"

He turned to King Rolf, puzzled by the sick look about him. "But, sire — it is *magnificent,* do you not see? We could travel unmolested anywhere — to the ends of the earth! It is safe passage even through the Turmaks. Ah, sir! — do not stand on ceremony now."

"A — a contagion wagon?" The King could scarcely say the words.

"The *semblance* of one," Timon said.

But the King did not hear. He sank to the ground and covered his eyes with his hand.

"Have you forgotten so soon?" he said. "There was a time one could not go out without seeing people writhing in the streets with blackened twisted faces, and the wagons end to end upon all the roads. Even now, few as they are, they move like coffins taking their pitiful cargo to die in remote places. The black flag like some evil bird and the dry tinkling of the bell like the tintinnabulation of Hell's own dinner bell. It is *not* exquisite or magnificent." With a small choke he rose and shut himself in the carriage.

The Bear and the Jester looked at each other and away. The Bear sat against the stone and stared at the ground. Timon squatted where he was, tearing up blades of brown grass. The only sound was the buzz of insects.

"I have not heard the King speak at such length since the curse," Timon said. The Bear said nothing and the silence continued.

They turned slowly at the creak of the carriage door. The King came out. He looked shaken. "We must do it, I suppose," he said.

"I think so, sire," Timon said.

The King ran his hand across his eyes. "Then we will. Is there anything more?"

The Bear's mouth opened and a hesitant look came upon him.

"Something else you think will upset me?" the King asked.

"In case we are stopped I should be covered with a blanket or cloth, like a victim already dead, while the King plays the part of a sick man. This would scare off anyone bold enough to doubt us."

The King's face turned pasty again. Eventually he nodded. "The logic is clear," he whispered. "And I must put black splotches on my face and hands." He looked from one to the other and said with a weak smile, "Well, we will see which of us does better — Timon as an ordinary fellow or myself as a victim of the plague."

They rested until dark and then were on the road again and passed without incident through the border barrier that the Queen's men had not guarded since the annexation.

That they had crossed out of the cursed kingdom was evident immediately. The night breeze was cool, the grass sweet and yielding as they walked beside the road. Full trees cast shadows in the moonlight.

The carriage was shoved into a thick stand of bushes near the first town and in the morning Timon went to make the necessary transactions.

He returned driving a gray mare and a dilapidated wagon with the message *Terhune — Baker & Confectioner* painted across its sides.

The Bear stared. He was so shocked he could only motion with his paws toward the wagon until finally he sputtered, "It's *open* in front and back!"

"Was I going to make the rounds of the town asking if anyone knew of a contagion wagon for sale?" Timon said. "No, no — our contagion wagon must have no history. There was a prison wagon which would have done splendidly — exactly the right construction and spirit — but no one is going to be able to say 'This contagion wagon looks like the old prison wagon and this driver looks like the fellow who bought it.' There's old wood in it, and tools. We will alter this to what we need."

The Bear stared a while longer. Then he began to nod slowly and finally murmured, "This is exactly right."

On the third morning the Bear stuffed his portmanteau into the secret compartment he had constructed under one corner of the roof, and the drab wagon rolled into the fog to begin its slow, dreadful journey toward the Green Hills.

A grim unshaven peasant drove, looking neither left nor right as the jingle of the little bell sent its warning through the hills and emptied the road. Mothers swept their children behind skirts, strong men made signs and murmured incantations, and soldiers rode a wide arc off the road to pass.

Inside, the King lay on his cot. Usually he was lost in fantasies of the Princess but sometimes even these were not enough to distract him from the jolting and the close air and his memories of the plague. Then he would drag himself up and ask the Bear for a game of backgammon.

Games obviously bored the Bear, and from the start he had ignored both the discomfort and the King. But he never refused King Rolf's plea. Nor did he show impatience at the King's slow play.

They avoided towns when they could and never did business in them. Instead, a small old fellow with a beard appeared in town at sundown. He purchased food and often stopped at an inn or tavern, listening for news concerning themselves and asking discreet questions of April Flower's whereabouts.

In the evenings Timon and the King chatted idly while the Bear sat aside mulling over his own affairs. So distant did he seem that they were surprised when he interjected one evening in a wistful voice, "Merth? You have been to Merth, King? They say it is beautiful. I was going there before —" He paused and even in the pale firelight Timon could see his slight frown. "Before I decided to go to the Plain of Waving Grass," he finished.

"Merth is beautiful," the King said. "And the Dowager is goodhearted, if somewhat boring. I will give you letters of introduction if you wish."

"Why go to the Plain?" Timon asked. "I have never heard it called anything but mildly pleasant."

The Bear looked at him quickly, an unreadable penetrating look. Then he shrugged. "I scarcely know. A clairvoyant accosted me and said in that shamelessly dramatic voice they affect: *Go to the Plain of Waving Grass.* No doubt she has said it to dozens of others and there may be a stream of us headed for the Plain. I suppose I go out of curiosity."

Timon snorted. "A good thing she did not say *Wear a pink tunic and carry sunflowers.*"

"And a good thing for you, Fool, that I am so good-natured."

"Is *that* what it is called?"

The Bear let out an appreciative roar of laughter. "Fool, your epitaph will read: *Slain for a joke.*"

Timon shrugged. "Better that than: *Expired tongue-tied.*"

With another laugh the Bear walked into the dark. A few minutes later Timon heard him flinging pebbles into the nearby stream.

The next morning brought another dense fog. Moisture dripped from the trees and their voices were eerily muted.

Timon slipped down to fill the water jug that was kept under the driver's seat, while the Bear and King Rolf tended to other last-minute chores. As he leaned over to dip the jug into the stream his glance was caught by a large dark shape he had not noticed the night before. He squinted. The shape did not move, so he filled the jug and had started up the bank when he heard a faint unearthly groan.

No mistaking where it came from!

He stared at the shape. It didn't move but it moaned again.

51

He went closer, wishing furiously for the fog to lift so that he could see — *whatever it was* without going nearer. But the fog paid his wish no heed.

It was about the bulk of — he leaned closer — the Bear!

A strangled croak.

A large limb was flung up and thudded back to the stones.

Timon stood rooted. When nothing more happened he took a shallow breath and went nearer.

He bent over the shape. It radiated warmth and wore a fur coat — or was furry.

"A bear!" he gasped.

He scrambled up the bank to get help, and soon the dancing bear was bent over the still form.

"Well, he's got arrows in him — that's all," the Bear said in a voice trembling with rage. "Get the King — we'll need his help."

The unconscious bear was half-carried, half-dragged up the bank and finally hoisted into the wagon and onto the Bear's cot. Except for a few ghastly moans he showed no sign of life until the Bear snapped the arrow shafts close to the wounds. The hot body convulsed and would have rolled off if they had not held it. Then the eyes opened — wet, fevered dark pools, and he whispered hoarsely inaudible words.

Timon handed the Bear a cup of water, which he held to the creature's lips. He swallowed some, some dribbled down his chin.

"Don't try to talk," the Bear said. "You're with friends."

But the bear would not be still. The cup was no sooner taken away than the lips began to work again. The Bear leaned his ear close, then said, "He wants to be taken to Ley — a physician called Ley. Do you know him?"

Both the King and Timon shook their heads.

The wounded bear clutched his forearm and tried to speak.

Finally the Bear pieced together enough information to give Timon directions. "Careful," he added. "The man is a known bear-sympathizer and may be watched."

Timon's eyes roved across the landscape, pausing at clumps of bush and out-croppings of rock, but he saw nothing suspicious and before long the physician's cottage came into view. It was at the edge of a dell, isolated and shaded by two enormous oaks. As the wagon rolled near the cottage Timon saw a face peer out from behind a lifted curtain. Surprise and alarm twisted its features. The curtain fell into place and soon an elderly man ran out.

"Ley?" Timon asked.

"Ley," the man repeated. "You need help?"

Timon jumped down and spoke in a low voice. "You are alone?"

The physician nodded, his expression perplexed.

Without a word Timon led him to the back of the wagon. The door was unbolted from the inside and flung open.

Ley's eyes widened. "Two!" he cried.

"One badly wounded," the Bear said.

Instantly the physician recovered from his shock and climbed in. With practiced hands he examined the bear.

"Draw up as close to my door as you can," he said to Timon finally, rubbing his hand across his eyes as he stepped down. "When the bears are inside, take the wagon into the shed —" He motioned toward the small building at the back of the yard.

"If it is in plain sight others will stay away," Timon said.

"No doubt," Ley replied with a rueful smile. "But contagion wagons travel relentless paths. Too much stopping will raise alarm."

There was no arguing that.

All four lifted the wounded bear out of the wagon and into the cottage. When Timon had hidden the wagon, he returned to find the Bear pacing the floor in front of the sickroom and the King slouched in a chair dabbing his forehead with a damp cloth. He had cleaned the black spots from his face.

The Bear glanced at Timon. "My portmanteau!" he exclaimed.

"You have not been robbed," Timon said with slight scorn for the unbecoming appearance of the Bear's mercenary streak.

Without a word the creature went out. He returned with the bag just as Ley came out of the other room. The physician's expression told enough.

"Good!" the Bear said. There was such relief in his voice that Timon could scarcely believe this was the same fellow who, only minutes earlier, had been so concerned with his riches.

"He wishes to see you all."

They crowded into the small room.

"So stupid," the bear said with a weak smile. "I don't deserve my good luck — your help. I wandered too far into the low hills." He turned his face to the wall and broke into a spasm of coughing.

"Don't talk. We're glad we were there," the Bear said when the coughing had subsided.

But the bear in the bed was staring at the other and could not contain his curiosity. "*Why are you here?*"

The Bear glanced at Ley, who shook his head slightly. "The

54

physician frowns," the Bear said. "I'll come in and bore you with the story after you've rested."

The wounded bear started to protest but succumbed to his weakness and nodded. As they filed out the Bear went back to the bed. "One thing we must know now. This hunter — is he following you, do you think?"

A look of satisfaction lit the other bear's eyes and he shook his head. "I killed him."

"Ah," was the Bear's only reply. When they had left the bear to sleep he said, "At least that one will not follow us here."

"What fools they are," Ley said. "They hang about the fringes of the bears' habitats hoping to catch one alone, and will never hunt together because they do not wish to divide the reward. This hunter's fate is a common one." The physician was watching the King. "There is a concealed room in the cellar. We will take him down later." Without a change of tone he said, "You are King Rolf. And you —" he looked at Timon "— are the Jester. Do you know Vos has offered a reward for you?"

Timon shrugged. "I am not surprised. A reward for us both or only the King?"

"Both."

The Jester laughed. "I'm glad to hear it — they had no call to insult me." The Bear gave a snort.

"They look for the Royal Carriage and say a large widow may be in the party." When Timon snickered the physician looked at him and then, incredulously, at the Bear. "You do not mean —"

"I fear so," the Bear said with no trace of humor.

Ley tried unsuccessfully to hide his amusement as he began laying out a handsome supper. Afterward they sat before the fire so full they could scarcely speak.

Finally Ley said, "You are a dancer, are you not, Bear?"

"I am," came the proud but lazy voice.

"And yet —" Ley leaned forward and peered closer at him. "You limp, and I suspect, you were once badly lame. You will excuse my impertinence —," he added quickly. "A professional interest. Who was the surgeon?"

The Bear exploded into warm laughter. "The surgeon Felton," he said. "A fiddler I was with many years. Your professional eye is discerning, physician. I was born lame, or injured very young — I don't know which. Felton came upon me hobbling alone, no more than a few weeks old. Abandoned, obviously." He said it without bitterness. "He didn't quite cure the leg, but you see the lameness is scarcely noticeable." He laughed again. "I believe he broke the leg and put it back together differently."

"Amazing!" Ley exclaimed. "A fiddler! A natural —"

Suddenly there was a light rapping at the door.

Without even showing his surprise the Bear disappeared into the other room.

"A patient," Ley assured Timon and the King. He glanced carefully at the door the Bear had closed, then opened the front door as the knocking was repeated.

It was clear to Timon, sitting in the shadows, that Ley did not know the extremely thin man who stood on his doorstep with his hair puffed out like a small bush.

The man smiled pleasantly.

Timon stiffened.

A wide space separated the stranger's front teeth.

He brought his hands from behind his back and made a small bow. He was holding a green hat.

Chapter Seven

*J*arvis is my name.
    Good evening, all the same.

Ley's brow wrinkled in surprise. "The same to you, friend. What can I do for you?"

The stranger turned his hat in his hand, smiled and nodded briefly at Timon.

A student of bears I be,
Engaged in writing their history.
Chapter eight —
On their fate
Since the great Persecution
Has been in execution.
Can you give me a clue?
I pray you do.

Ley stared at him a long while. "No one here is interested in bears," he said at last in an even tone. "Now, good night to you, sir."

Jarvis blinked and pressed his hand against the door as it was closing in his face. Timon braced himself for more verse but the poet said, "I was sure there was a certain — *bearness* about this place."

57

"Well, there is *no* bearness about this place," Ley said with rising impatience. "I have not seen a bear in years — and will be content never to see another. And you will do well to obey the Queen's law too. Have you never heard of the Law Forbidding the Perpetuation of the Memory of Bears? A *history* of bears! Could anything be more against that law?"

The stranger gaped at him. Then he gathered himself up indignantly.

You lie, sir!
Fie, sir!

He paused and once again verse failed him. "I know nothing of the law here but I have seen how the Queen plasters the walls and trees and fences with likenesses of the bear."

"That is so we will not forget the face of the enemy," Ley explained blandly.

"A perverse way to erase the memory of them!"

The physician heard this sensible observation without expression. "You will not provoke me to criticize the Queen," he said. "Good-bye, sir."

I would have sworn
A certain bearness was borne
By this gentle house — er —

He thoughtfully put his finger against the side of his nose as the door was shutting him out. *"By this gentle house forlorn."*

Ley put his ear to the door and soon came away shaking his head. "A *poet*-spy!" he exclaimed with a smile. "And such a *bad* poet! What will Vos not try next? His spies have tried to make me drunk so that they could draw subversive words out of me. They have come saying they love bears and wish to help them — by helping *me* to help them."

The Bear came out. "You saw?" Timon said.

The Bear shook his head.

He heard the news without comment, then slipped out the back. Ley did not hide his surprise but asked no questions.

"This spy is extremely inept," Timon said. "Or extremely subtle."

"Am I too cynical?" Ley asked. "He does not have the air about him of the usual spy."

"Then surely he *is* one," Timon said. "But in truth, if I did not know he had been to the castle asking about the Bear, nothing would convince me he is anything but what he says. *By this gentle house — er — forlorn!*"

The Bear came back. "He's going west over the hill toward a curl of smoke. Your neighbor?"

Ley nodded.

"Maybe he senses a certain bearness there too," Timon said.

"Then his sense misleads him," Ley said. "He heads for a new cottage that no bear has been near."

Timon sobered. "Was it this *sense* that kept him from going to Sanring?"

The next morning they got the wounded bear into the cellar and while the two bears talked the others prepared for the departure. Timon was glad they had found the bear. He did not begrudge the time this detour had taken. But when he saw the King's languorous movements and remembered how tired he had

59

been himself the night before, he was anxious to be underway again.

Besides, he had dreamed of the poet-spy.

Was he following them, or had mere coincidence taken him to the two places where the Bear had stopped?

He nearly cried out with exasperation when the Bear came out of the cellar and said to Ley, "He says you will get him across the border. Can I help? I will stay awhile if I can be useful."

To Timon's bounding relief, Ley shook his head. "My friends and I have done this many times. We will see him safely out."

The Bear nodded quickly, accepting the physician's words. He reached for his portmanteau, and Timon thought he was at last ready to leave.

But he was wrong.

The Bear stuck his paw into the bag. He paused that way for a moment and then said, "Take this."

The startling thought crossed Timon's mind that the Bear was about to give Ley part of the Royal Jewels.

Wrong again.

The Bear's paw came up full of gold coins. Timon's eyes started, but no more than did the King's and Ley's.

He put the gold on the table, reached into the bag again and brought out a like pile, which he put beside the first.

"For medicines," he said. "Or to bribe a soldier or a spy."

Ley did not hesitate. "Thank you," he said in an astounded voice. "We all thank you."

The Bear shrugged and went out to the wagon, leaving the others to follow in stunned silence.

Timon drove in the deepest abstraction.

What other unsuspected riches were in the bag?

A curious kind of miser who would give away so much. Unasked! But if he were *not* so miserly, why was he risking his life to get the Royal Jewels?

The Jester was so preoccupied with the Bear's contradictory character that the gap-toothed spy nearly rode by unnoticed.

The green hat caught Timon's eye, and he nearly leapt out of the seat. Then he hunched over and watched as Jarvis trotted around them, giving the wagon the wide berth all riders gave it. Obviously he did not recognize Timon.

When he was a speck in the road Timon said in a voice that could be heard inside the wagon, "The spy has just ridden by, going in the same direction we do."

Neither the Bear nor the King commented.

After that the driver of the contagion wagon seemed as bent-over and dozing as before but his eyes roved constantly, seeking out a green hat.

No more was seen of it until two nights later.

Timon pushed open the door of the noisiest inn and stared across the room with a sinking heart. There was Jarvis, leaning across a table, earnestly talking to a burly man with a beard coarse as black briars. Timon realized he had begun to believe they had seen the last of the spy.

Secure in his disguise, he approached within eavesdropping distance and had barely reached the table next to them when the man slammed his tankard to the table and shouted, "Blithering fool! Get away from me!"

"But, sir —," Jarvis began, his face expressing hurt surprise.

"Nobody talks to me about bears!" the man said loudly. He

61

looked around, obviously hoping to be heard clearly by soldiers or lurking spies. "Get away from me!"

The man seized up his tankard and with a scornful "Aargh!" went to the other side of the room.

Timon sat. He considered opening his conversation with Jarvis by warning him how foolish it was to talk of bears here but changed his mind. Best to ease into the subject.

He leaned toward Jarvis, who was staring disconsolately into his cup. "I have been admiring your hat, sir," he said in a raspy low voice that fit his aged appearance.

Jarvis looked up eagerly.

You like this hat of mine?
Perhaps I'll ask you to dine,
Fine sir!
Wine, sir?

He offered Timon his cup of ale.

"I can compliment a man's choice of hats without taking dinner in return," Timon said. He moved to the seat opposite Jarvis. "But I see you are to be complimented further. You are a poet."

The thin face lit up, but before he could reply in either verse or plain words, a great commotion rose at the entrance. Two soldiers pushed in with swords drawn.

Then came the captain who had stopped them on the road. Timon stifled the impulse to duck into the shadows. Why call attention to himself? He casually propped his elbows on the table and when the captain's glance fixed on him momentarily his eyes did not waver.

A dough-faced man with tiny eyes peered around the captain. "Him!" he shouted, pointing at Jarvis. "Asking questions about bears! Saying he is a scholar! Writing a history of bears! If this does not earn me my reward, I want to know what will!"

"What is he talking about?" Jarvis sputtered as the Queen's men advanced on him. "I have never seen this man in my life."

"But he has heard you," the captain said. He turned to the informer. "You sat — where?"

The man clapped his hand at the place where Timon had sat a minute ago. "*Do you know where there are bears?* he asked. *What was it like when the Queen's prohibition began?* and *Who knows most about bears?*"

"In short, tried to provoke others to think of bears and to talk about them," the captain said. He turned on Jarvis. "Have you a defense?"

Jarvis stared at them in amazement. Then he drew up his thin frame. "What if I have done these things?" he challenged. "I am a scholar. I have done nothing unreasonable."

The captain's eyes widened. "It is unreasonable to break the Law Forbidding the Perpetuation of the Memory of Bears."

As Jarvis opened his mouth Timon was inexplicably seized with the impulse to cry out to him *Apologize! Swear it will not happen again!* He swallowed hard and bit the inside of his lip.

"I have heard of that law," Jarvis said. "I thought the man was having a *joke* at my expense. You are not telling me such a preposterous law actually exists!"

"Preposterous!" the Queen's men roared together. Everyone else sat in shocked silence except the informer, who squealed with glee at each incriminating word.

Recovering from their surprise, the soldiers lunged toward Jarvis, but the captain held up his hand.

"Not so hastily," he purred. "We must let this — reasonable gentleman — explain himself. Now, sir — tell us just how the Law Forbidding the Perpetuation is preposterous."

Jarvis nodded. "Nothing will give me more pleasure." Timon jammed his fist against his mouth to keep from shouting at the imbecile. "It is preposterous," Jarvis continued placidly, "because at every turn the Queen reminds her subjects of bears. Their pictures are everywhere. Enormous rewards dangle irresistibly in front of every man's eyes."

As Jarvis talked the captain's eyes glinted with mounting satisfaction. "In short, the Queen and her people act foolishly?"

"Of course they do!" Jarvis said. "It is incredibly foolish!"

A smug smile curled the captain's lips. "Well, well — you must tell these things to the Queen herself." He motioned to his men to seize the culprit. "More than anything, she and Vos enjoy being called *preposterous* and *foolish*!"

"I *know* he is a spy," Timon said, dusting pie crumbs from his hands. "But as I listened to him putting a noose around his own neck and then calmly pulling it tighter and tighter, I *forgot*. He seemed a kind of — *brave idiot*, and I was tempted to save him." He glanced up at the Bear, expecting to see an expression of scorn.

"What is this? — fondness?" was the Bear's unexpected comment.

Timon blinked. "No," he said. "Only misplaced sympathy." Suddenly a shudder went through him. "The curse is addling my brain, you see," he said in a flat voice. "The entire episode was probably a charade concocted between them to draw out fools like me."

"But you revealed nothing." The Bear picked up the portmanteau, which he had brought out of its niche, and began prying and picking with his claws at the lock and hinges to be sure they were secure. He had already done this several times since their journey began. Timon watched with fascination, remembering how this same Bear had plunked two great piles of gold on Ley's table and had left them without a backward glance. "He told you nothing before he was taken away?" the Bear asked without looking up.

"The soldiers came too soon. He is asking where the bears are and who knows them."

"Well," the Bear said, "if he is not a spy he'll rot in the Queen's dungeon and be no danger to us. If he is a spy —" He shrugged. "We will see. Did you learn anything of where we find the clairvoyant?"

"Nothing except that it is five days to the border and the Green Hills."

"Good news at last!"

Timon looked at him askance. "So happy you are happy," he said. "If April Flower is in them, we must go, but I do not look forward to the privilege."

His words needed no explanation. The Bear and King Rolf knew as well as he did that just beyond the Queen's land — like a great impenetrable barrier — the Green Hills stretched mile upon mile east, west, north. Broken and eroded by the freezes at night and the baking by day and the cutting winds that blew all seasons. A place of narrow passes and canyons that looked promising to the traveler but ended at the foot of sheer cliffs, barren tablelands that must be climbed and crossed or circumvented by obscure and tortuous trails, rubble-strewn slopes that mocked sure-footed animals. All of it naked except for brittle under-growth.

They were called the Green Hills because they were not — the bitter joke of some defeated traveler.

In the silence that followed, Timon's mind filled with all the unpleasant tales he had heard of the Green Hills, and when the Bear spoke he was surprised to realize the creature's thoughts had not dwelt at all on that subject.

"You are certain he did not know you," the Bear said.

"Certain," Timon said, finally bringing his thoughts back. "The spy thinks me a fine, friendly fellow."

But the certainty flew three nights later when he walked a market street and saw the green hat in the entrance of a tavern. Their eyes met and the poet nodded with an intent, puzzled ex-pression, as if he were trying to remember something important.

He started toward Timon, who nodded and turned quickly into an alley. Darting up the passage, Timon listened for footsteps but did not pause to see if Jarvis followed. He left the town by a circuitous route, dodging through dark lanes and climbing fences, and finally returned to the wagon by walking very far around.

"He's free," he announced, sinking dejectedly beside the fire. "Obviously the soldiers knew when they saw him that he was a spy — as I said, or he informed them as soon as they were alone. And tonight he knew me. Not as someone casually familiar. I was — *interesting* to him."

"Perhaps because you praised his poetry the other night," the King said, giving Timon a cup of wine.

The Bear chortled but was silent a long time. Finally he said, "We'll have to kidnap him."

The cup fell from Timon's hand. The King's chin dropped.

Then Timon began to laugh. "You've done it again! How do we do it?"

"*You* do it," the Bear said.

Timon stared. He opened his mouth but no words came. Then he swallowed and gestured carelessly.

"That's generous," he said blandly. "Any special way you'd like it done?"

The Bear had no suggestion for the moment.

As the shock wore off Timon saw that the kidnapping must fall to him. Who else could move about freely, seek out the spy and —*what?* Bludgeon him unconscious and drag him back in the dinner sack?

The three ate in silence.

"All right," Timon said suddenly. "The Queen's lackey is interested in me? Then I will present myself to him. I'll go back and find him, make certain he sees me, then allow him to follow me here. Or if he takes a friendly approach and speaks to me, I'll invite him to — my *cottage* for supper. To meet my good wife and babies. We overpower him, truss him up, and throw him into the wagon until we decide what to do with him. Most of all," he added hastily, "we *gag* him."

He looked from the Bear to King Rolf and back.

"The simplicity recommends it," the Bear said.

"But what if he has confederates concealed?" the King said.

Timon gave him a reproachful look. "I did not need to hear that, King."

They lapsed into silence again.

"There is no other way," Timon said finally. "I will simply have to — deal with whatever comes."

"I think he would not have you arrested so soon," the Bear said thoughtfully. "More useful to him to stay with you a while — let you incriminate yourself and lead him to —"

He made a quick, silencing gesture and darted into the dark. Before Timon and the King could recover from their surprise they heard a cry and scuffling. Then the Bear reappeared and tossed a figure into the dirt by the fire.

Chapter Eight

The green hat flew off and landed in the fire.

"You!" Timon cried. "You *followed* me? *Followed* me?"
After all his wiles! He had never been so disappointed in his life!
He felt like picking the flaming hat out of the fire and setting it
on the spy's head!

Jarvis scrambled up, reaching toward the fire. Then, with a
pained expression, gave up on the hat.

"No!" he said. "Not the way you mean!"

"What other way is there?" Timon snapped.

"I — *sensed* where you were. I came straight."

Timon gave a growl of disbelieving disgust. "Did you bring
others?"

The spy shook his head.

I would have made myself known
Had this bear not broken my bone.

"Broken your bone?" the Bear repeated with surprise.

Jarvis gave a weak laugh. "Well, not actually."

"I see," the bear said drily. "It rhymes."

The spy shrugged apologetically.

On the spur of the moment, you know,
Greatness is slow to flow.

"You don't say." The Bear gestured impatiently. "Enough of

69

this nonsense. What are you doing here? What do you mean you *sensed* where the Fool was?"

"Just that. I am looking for a particular bear and when I saw your friend this evening I suddenly sensed a certain —"

"*Bearness?*"

Jarvis's eyes widened at the Bear's interruption. "Exactly. Of course I did not guess that he would actually lead me to a bear. That he had been somehow associated with bears — that is all I sensed. And I must confess my — intuition is very often wrong. If you knew the rebuffs and troubles I have earned by approaching the wrong people."

"As you did at the tavern two nights ago," Timon said. "We know you are a spy, Jarvis! Do not think you will leave here to inform on the Bear."

Jarvis blinked. "A spy?" He stared at Timon's hardened features and at the expressionless Bear. He looked at King Rolf, who stared back. "No, no!" he cried. "What makes you think that?" He turned to Timon. "You saw me accused and carried out by the Queen's men."

"And tonight you are free."

"Oh!"

"Yes — oh!"

To their surprise the man began to laugh. "They released me," he said finally, still smiling. He dusted himself off and sat near the fire.

Will you spare me some wine?
How I thirst for the fruit of the vine.
Sumptuous red, sparkling white —
Anything at all will be my delight.

The Bear snatched up the wine jug. "Only on your oath to spout no more rhyme."

The poet gave him a baleful look. "What? But I —"

"Swear! — or I give you wine over the top of your head."

"But I — all right. I will do my best, but —"

"No buts."

Jarvis swallowed and nodded. "You dislike poetry?" he asked tentatively.

"I dislike poetry when it is so b—" The Bear looked down at the disappointed face. "I dislike it when it is so slow and other matters are urgent. Now explain why you are not in some dungeon." He gave Jarvis a cup and filled it.

"I told them I was a clairvoyant."

Timon felt the Bear stiffen.

"Of course they doubted me — just as you do — but I was able to tell them a few things about themselves that I had no other way of knowing, and they were convinced. Even the captain. They let me go because they are like most — afraid of clairvoyants. Think we cast spells, summon up earthquakes and storms at will — such things. They wished to keep on my good side — and here I am."

"You *are* a clairvoyant?" the Bear asked.

"Of extremely minimal powers," Jarvis said. "Any clairvoyant with more — developed powers, would have known instantly that this gentleman —" he motioned toward Timon "— is associated with bears. But see how late I realized that fact.

"Also, I have messages for a certain bear and I feel he has come this way. But intuition tells me nothing of where to find him. So I search for someone who knows — either where this particular bear is, or who else might help me find him. I look at a

71

man and sense he might know. I speak to him. He gets very angry because I broach the forbidden subject, and says he knows nothing about bears. Maybe he lies, maybe he doesn't. *I* can never be sure."

"You *felt* there was a bear at King Rolf's castle?" Timon asked.

"Yes. They said I was mistaken but I was not entirely convinced. I set off to find the King himself at a place called Sanring but halfway there something told me I was going in the wrong direction. All the wasted time!" He looked up sharply. "How do you know I was there?"

"My people sent word," the King said. The others did not try to silence him, being convinced the man told the truth. No one, Timon thought, would *invent* such a vague clairvoyant.

"Ah!" Jarvis made a slight bow then turned to Timon. "And the Jester. They are looking for you, you know. The reward is —"

"This bear you are looking for," the Bear interrupted. "What bear?"

Jarvis's eyes lit. "Of course! You may even *know* him! A crippled bear."

"I am that bear," the Bear said, breaking the long silence.

"Oh, no," Jarvis said shaking his head. "This bear is *quite* crippled. You scarcely limp."

"I am that bear," the Bear repeated with rising impatience. "My leg was — fixed. What a desperate lot you clairvoyants are! Dragged off the street by those two, and now you come. Did they tell you they got not the fraction of a kliner from me?"

"I have never met them," Jarvis said calmly, "but I am not surprised others have received messages about you."

"They were not looking for a crippled bear."

"Probably they discerned about you what I could not — that even though your impairment is slight now, you are the one."

"What messages?" the Bear asked with scorn. "Am I to take five hundred thousand kliner to the Plain instead of three hundred thousand? Or —" he glanced at Timon "— wear a pink tunic and carry sunflowers?"

"This is no frivolous matter," Jarvis said. "And I think, though you deny it to yourself and others, you know it is not frivolous. Are you not headed for the Plain? And do you not carry a small fortune?"

"I am turning miserly," the Bear said angrily. "And I go to the Plain from curiosity."

"You go to the Plain with three hundred thousand kliner to free your father from the Plains Turmaks."

The Bear's paw closed around the clairvoyant's throat and lifted him off the ground.

"What?" he whispered.

Jarvis coughed and tried to pry the claws open.

"He can't talk," Timon said.

The Bear's head jerked around and he stared at Timon as if he were a stranger. Then he blinked and let go. "If this is a trick," he said in a hoarse undertone, "you will be sorry indeed."

Jarvis rubbed his throat.

Would I go through this for a trick?
As soon beat myself with a stick!

73

He yelped and jumped out of the Bear's reach. "Sorry!" Then he straightened and said defiantly, "Let me tell you I may have lost my place at the White Crane Inn by looking for you. Do you know what an inspiration such a place can be? — the room overhanging the river! Do you know how long is the waiting list for that room? If I do not get there soon they will give it to someone else. A trick?" He stepped up to the Bear. "Let me get this over with and be on my way. The rest of the message is that you are to find April Flower. She will tell you the details. Good-bye."

But the Bear clamped a paw on Jarvis's shoulder. "What do you know about my father? Where are these Turmaks?"

"He is their Fighting Bear," Jarvis said. "Chained and set upon by dogs and bullies to amuse village idiots and savages. But I —"

"Chained and set upon by dogs!" The Bear stared at him with rage. His claws dug into the poet's shoulder. "*Where?*"

"Let go!" Jarvis cried. "I don't know! I would tell you. Of course I would tell you."

The Bear loosened his grip and stared at the poet a long moment.

Then he turned to Timon and the King. "I must go to the Plain. I am sorry to break our agreement but — I must do this." He went into the wagon and came out with his bag. "The Royal Jewels are in the niche."

"You cannot, Bear," Timon said, rousing from his shock.

"I know what this journey means to you," the Bear said. "I am sorry —" He made a helpless gesture. "What else can I say? I must do this. You go to April Flower. I will find her after — my father is free, and we will go to the Queen."

"You have three hundred thousand kliner?" Jarvis asked.

The Bear turned on him angrily and threw down the portmanteau. Coins jingled inside it, but they all knew this was not the jingle of three hundred thousand kliner.

"I will not need *kliner* to take care of my father's captors!"

"Of course you must go," Timon said, "but where? The Plain is a big place. How much time you will waste searching! This man says April Flower can tell you more. In two days we cross the border."

"Her powers are strong," Jarvis said admiringly.

"We will travel day and night," Timon said. "Even if the moon were not full you would be safer in the wagon. Soldiers are everywhere — looking for the King and me."

The Bear growled and stalked into the dark.

The King cleared his throat. "Do you — *sense* anything for the Princess and myself?" he asked.

Jarvis considered and shook his head regretfully. "You have no idea, King, how *inadequate* a clairvoyant I am."

"Thank you anyway," the King murmured, then walked away, his disappointment obvious in the droop of his shoulders.

"And you know nothing of the Dancing Bear who can lift the curse from us?" Timon asked.

The clairvoyant's brow wrinkled. He closed his eyes and pressed his fingers against them. Then, as Timon expected, he shook his head.

The Bear returned and grudgingly agreed Timon was right.

Soon Jarvis was jogging up a hill in the direction of the White Crane Inn and the contagion wagon rolled northward at an unseemly fast clip.

Chapter Nine

Their speed was never enough for the Bear. He growled with frustration when Timon reminded him what suspicions a speeding contagion wagon would rouse, but did not argue. Ahead, heat rose out of the Green Hills in shimmering waves.

Timon no longer went into town but instead bought food from farmhouses and cottages near the road. King Rolf and the Bear ate in the wagon and Timon dined in snatches as he drove. They stopped in the early morning hours, slept until daylight, and then were on the road again. Each day Timon was more and more fatigued and hard pressed to keep awake on the driver's seat.

He paid no attention when a band of soldiers approached at dusk of the evening before they were to cross the border, and made the usual detour to avoid the wagon.

Suddenly he realized they had stopped and one was shouting at him. "Look you! Contagion wagon! Hoa!"

He jerked up, brought the wagon to a stop. "They're keeping their distance," he said in an undertone that could be heard inside. "Whyfor?" he shouted to the soldiers.

One of them, scarcely more than a silhouette in the fading light, rose in his saddle and cupped his hands to his mouth.

"Stay away from the town tomorrow! The Princess passes through!"

A sharp cry came from inside the wagon.

Timon waved. "Done!"

The soldiers moved on, and he flicked the whip over the mare's back, cursing them. What wild, longing thoughts had they put into the King's head?

When they finally pulled the wagon behind thick shrubs hidden from the road by a small rise, the King was silent. After several futile attempts to rouse him from his melancholy, both Timon and the Bear left him to his solitude. Soon he mumbled a negligent "Good night" and retired.

"I wish he had not heard that," the Bear said in a surly tone.

"It adds nothing to his happiness," Timon said, glancing at the still form rolled in the blanket.

"His happiness is not what I had in mind." The Bear doused the fire and went to the other side of the wagon.

The next morning Timon was wakened by violent shaking and pain shooting through his shoulder and arm. It was barely light.

"What's the matter with you?" he screamed at the Bear as he beat at the paw digging into his flesh.

The Bear's grip only tightened. He leaned his face close to Timon's.

"Your precious King has bestirred himself and *flown*," he said in a voice seething with rage. "He has flown on the horse and I think we don't need to ask where."

He waved a black-smeared rag in Timon's face.

"He has wiped off his plague and gone to court his Princess." The Bear's voice shook. Timon thought he would burst with his anger. "A plague on him! I will wring his neck if I see him again! I will kill him!"

Timon sat on the ground trying to chase the night's fuzziness from his brain, trying to get a grip on the disaster the morning had brought.

"He couldn't," he said. "How could he do all that?" He threw the rag onto the ashes of the dead fire. "It's all he can do to wake up in the morning. And he hasn't ridden a horse in years."

"It seems his *passion* surmounts his indolence," the Bear said with scathing sarcasm. "I told you he was dangerous. Imbecile lovestruck —"

Scarcely hearing the Bear, Timon cut in, "I must go after him. He might have been thrown. He could be hurt. He can't —" He jerked on his boots. "I'll get a ride."

The Bear grasped his arm. "You will get another horse and drive this wagon across the border," he growled, his mouth half an inch from Timon's ear.

Timon looked at him in astonishment.

"Leave the King? You're out of your mind."

"He will find us."

"He cannot take care of himself."

"Then there are those who will."

"Who?"

The two stared defiantly at each other.

"*Anyone*," the Bear said finally. "Anyone who comes upon that poor helpless imbecile will help him."

"He will tell them who he is," Timon shouted. "And when he is given to the Queen for the reward he will be ridiculed again, only worse, and sent back to his castle to turn to dust — under guard this time. Or he will be kept prisoner at the Crystal Palace and come to the same end.

"Or if he does not tell who he is, he will be taken for a vagrant and treated like one."

"And will that kill him?" the Bear asked with heavy sarcasm.

"Can you say it will not?" Timon barked. "You who have always taken care of yourself? So strong you can terrorize any man to do your bidding! A simple thing for *you* to say *will it kill him!*"

All this the Bear seemed not to hear. He caught Timon up by the arms. "*You* did this, Fool! He was ready to stay behind, but *you* —"

Timon pushed his foot into the Bear's stomach and found himself thrown to the grass. He scrambled up.

"I'll bring him back. It is a foolish thing for him to do, but —"

"Foolish!"

"All right — it is a stupid thing for him to do, but you know he cares for nothing but the Princess." He massaged the mauled shoulder and wondered there was not an open wound gushing blood. "I will bring him back and we'll be on our way."

The Bear turned on him. "No, Fool — you will get another horse and we will cross the border."

Timon shook his head vigorously. "No. You stay in the wagon. It is hidden from the road, and I will return soon."

The Bear did not reply, and Timon could see he was considering what else he could do.

"You cannot head for the border alone," Timon said. "There are too many soldiers, and the peasants will give alarm if they see you. I might find another horse, but force me to drive and I will drive to the town."

"I will not be here when you return," the Bear said, his voice shaking with anger.

As Timon headed toward the town the words turned in his mind. Had the Bear spoken out of anger — to scare him, or from a premonition? He could not shake off a growing foreboding. The country swarmed with the Queen's men and it was dangerous to leave the wagon sitting as it was, for contagion wagons traveled relentless paths and did not rest.

And yet there was such a fear of the wagon. Hadn't they seen it themselves every hour they were on the road? He would be back with the King long before anyone — soldier or peasant — screwed up the courage to approach the wagon.

He had no choice but to go after the King.

The road was full of people going to see the Princess. Soon he caught a ride, and as the cart jolted along, he expected to find the King collapsed beside the road.

He did not. Instead, he found King Rolf near the entrance to the town, craning his neck in the direction from which the Princess would come, oblivious of the crush of the boisterous townspeople who surrounded him. Timon shoved and squirmed until he was beside the King. He had never seen the King so flushed with excitement.

"King — are you all right?" he whispered loudly, tugging at the shabby cloak.

The King looked down at him and blinked, then recognized him. "So you could not stay away either!" he said.

"Sire, come! We must go back to — to you-know-who. He is in danger. We will see the Princess later."

King Rolf heard none of this. He shook off Timon's hand. "After so long I will finally see her again. Do you think she will recognize me in these sorry rags? I should have brought the crown." He looked down at Timon. "Why did I not think of that?"

Someone bumped against Timon's arm and a great pain shot through his shoulder.

"King — listen to me! We must —"

The King ignored him. "Madam, how much longer?" he impatiently asked the woman beside him.

She bounced her baby and shrugged. "They say she started later than she planned. Makes no difference to royalty when it starts or stops, does it?"

"Well, where is she coming from?"

"Everybody knows that," the woman said with surprise. "From the manor of the Baron Grist. They say she'll be betrothed to the Baron's son soon."

The King let out a cry. The woman looked alarmed and backed away.

"You heard that?" The King grasped Timon's sore arm.

"The woman doesn't know, sire!" Timon said desperately. "How could these people —"

"I must talk to the Princess!"

"No, King! That is the worst —"

His voice was drowned in a swell of cheers as the first riders of the Princess's party came into sight, pennants snapping in the breeze. The procession approached with a grand and elegant clanking, a shimmering of bridles, saddles, armor and weapons, and Timon knew the King would never be drawn away. His eyes shone as he drank in the splendor. Then the white coach came near, and he forgot all the rest.

The curtain was drawn back from the window and when King Rolf realized that the Princess was looking out toward the opposite side he cried, "Princess!"

Princess Jessy heard his voice amid all the others. She turned and there was no doubt that she recognized him. In fact, their eyes locked in such an embrace that both were oblivious of everything else. The coach moved along and the King ran beside it, talking in an urgent, imploring manner, unconsciously pushing aside any who blocked his way. Timon followed, receiving all the surly comments, the shoves and jabs. His eyes were not locked on the Princess but watched the soldiers ahead and behind. His only comfort was Vos's absence. When he saw a tall officer turn back and look hard and long at the ragtag figure running so persistently beside the coach, he pulled at the King.

"We can't stay here!" he said loudly into King Rolf's ear.

As well talk to a stone.

The soldier wheeled his horse and started toward them, shouting people out of his way.

"Come, sire!" Timon shouted. "This is dangerous!"

The King pushed him away without looking.

"Princess, who is this?" the officer asked, towering above them on the stamping horse. He stared intently down at the King.

Timon groaned and jumped between the Princess and the King.

"I apologize, Your Highness! I apologize most humbly!" he said, bowing to her. "He is in my charge. I looked away one moment and he was gone. He is —" He broke off and touched the side of his head. "But harmless. Harmless, I assure you." He turned to the soldier with an elaborate shrug. "He fancies he is royalty and in love with the Princess. No disrespect, Your Highness. It is —"

The King gaped at him and then Timon saw understanding come into his eyes. He looked at the officer. "Surpassing beautiful, is she not?" he said gaily. "Do you wonder I love her? Come with me, Princess. At my palace I have colored birds that sing love songs." He turned to Timon. "Will it be the gold coach or the silver? You choose — we are going to my palace."

"This is an outrage!" the officer barked. "Get this man away from the Princess and follow me!"

"Oh no, officer," the Princess said after a slight hesitation. "Surely that is not necessary. The poor man! He meant no harm. You —" She spoke to Timon. "Take him to his home — treat him well."

"Yes, Princess — certainly. Thank you! It will not happen again."

"See it does not!" the officer snapped. "Are you certain, Princess?"

She nodded.

"Very well," he said reluctantly. "Now get out of the road."

He signaled to the driver and the coach began to roll. Timon gave the King no time to look longingly after the Princess. Instead he dragged him back into the crowd. The King collapsed against a tree. Timon bit back the scathing remarks at the tip of his tongue and said only, "Where is the horse?"

As they made their way to the tavern where the King had pointed, Timon glanced at the sun and a feeling of dread washed over him.

So late! So late!

There is nothing to worry about, he told himself over and over again as they rode. A contagion wagon was safe anywhere. It was the symbol of Death to everyone. *Everyone.* Had he not seen this in all the faces they passed?

But his sense of foreboding only grew, and when they topped

the rise and saw the wagon standing in the open and people milling around it he cried out, "I knew it! I knew it!"

The wagon door hung open and children jumped in and out. As Timon watched, a girl climbed onto the driver's seat and rang the bell. It echoed through the air hollow and dry, more dreadful than any sound Timon had ever heard. He slid off as the mare approached a knot of chattering peasants.

"What's happened here?" he asked, for once reduced to the bare minimum of words.

They laughed. "Nobody knows," one of the men said. "Not us — and not them —" He pointed to three soldiers who stood near the wagon, glancing at it and shaking their heads.

"The wagon stood all morning behind the bushes," a woman said. "Some complained to the soldiers — it isn't what you want standing in the neighborhood, is it? — and finally the soldiers screwed up the courage to approach it." She gave a loud laugh. "Empty! An empty imitation contagion wagon!"

"How — odd," Timon said, barely getting the words out. Ignoring King Rolf, he went toward the wagon.

"May I look inside?" he asked the soldiers. They did not object.

Obviously the wagon had been closely searched. Clothes were strewn about and boards pried up. His eyes went to the secret compartment and he stifled a cry. Undisturbed!

He cast a surreptitious glance backward then slid it open. The portmanteau was gone! Whatever had happened, at least the Bear had been able to take the bag with him! Had he decided there was less danger in heading for the border undisguised than in staying in the standing wagon?

He looked about, wondering what to do next, then began rummaging through the tossed clothes he had only glanced at before. When he was done he let out a shout of laughter.

As quickly, he stifled the laugh and whispered, "Premature. Perhaps premature."

He jumped down from the wagon.

"Are you giving away the clothes?" he asked the soldiers.

"We give away nothing," one of them said.

"I thought you must have. All of that —" As he gestured scornfully toward the wagon his eye fixed on the flag stick. *Flagless.* He closed his eyes and sucked in his cheeks to keep back a ludicrous smile that would have to be explained. "So shabby," he finished.

The soldier hadn't noticed the pause. "Every stitch is there," he snapped. "We are not here to give gifts."

"Certainly not!" Timon agreed indignantly.

He ran back to the King, who had not moved. He was limp and still breathing in short gasps as he stared at the sight around the wagon.

"He's gone off dressed as the widow," Timon whispered. "No doubt going toward the border. Come!" He took the reins and laughed. "We'll catch up to him. She will want our company!"

Timon recognized the Bear walking beside the road long before they caught up to him. Then his eyes narrowed as he realized that the man alongside the veiled widow was not merely passing by but walking *with* her. The nearer they got, the more obvious it became that the two were acquainted. The man was even taller than the Bear, prosperous-looking and exquisitely dressed. He leaned toward the widow and spoke attentively. She nodded, made a reply. He threw back his head and laughed with delight.

Timon stared.

"It *is* him," he told the King, breaking into a giggle. "She has taken this giant's fancy. See how he tries to take her arm! I think we must rescue this lady."

He jumped down and led the horse abreast of the pair.

"Well met, cousin!" he cried, beaming at the veiled face. "I am sorry we were delayed." He looked up at the Bear's companion with an appreciative smile. "Our thanks, sir, for accompanying our cousin in our absence."

"Entirely my pleasure," the man said. His expression made clear that their arrival was no pleasure. "Your cousin is a remarkable and courageous woman, sir — undertaking such a journey so soon after her tragic loss."

"There is no woman like my cousin," Timon said.

The man agreed vociferously and would obviously have continued his compliments if the Bear had not interrupted. "This is Mr. Spang," he said in a voice high for a bear, deep for a lady, but certainly pleasing to Mr. Spang. "He is the best baker in the village across the border."

Mr. Spang's chest puffed out and he beamed at the Bear. "Now, Mrs. Hummingbird, I never said I was the best — though I can't deny it's true."

"Of course you are the best," Mrs. Hummingbird purred. "I could tell it immediately. I'm sure your tansy cake is superb — so few can bake a good tansy cake."

Timon turned away in a valiant attempt to keep sober. He failed. He began to choke and Mrs. Hummingbird gave him a thump across the back.

"Get hold of yourself, cousin," she said. She did not introduce her cousins to Mr. Spang, who was ready to ignore them altogether.

Timon finally recovered enough to speak. "Mr. Spang, I am sure we can take care of —" he nearly choked again "— *Mrs. Hummingbird* now. You look a man of many affairs — do not let us hold you."

He got a dark glower.

"Nothing is more important," Mr. Spang said, "than to be of service to —"

"*Must* you go?" Mrs. Hummingbird interrupted in sweet tones. "You have been such a comfort — but of course we cannot keep you — can we?"

Timon's chin dropped.

Mr. Spang's chest expanded again. "Certainly I will not leave your side so long as I can offer any jot of comfort."

Timon tugged at the widow's sleeve and whispered, "A word with you, cousin! Have you lost your mind?"

His cousin ignored him, and the party continued down the road toward the border.

At every step the widow heaped extravagant praise on Mr. Spang's wisdom, his appearance, his wit. He became so puffed up with his own superiority and so impressed with Mrs. Hummingbird's discriminating taste that Timon expected a marriage proposal any minute.

Timon himself was nearly silenced by hilarity and surprise. Why was the Bear bothering? Taking the chance of being unmasked by this self-important courtier with smudges of flour on his sleeve. *He* was not the one, Timon reflected with chagrin, to take foolish chances for a joke.

88

They came around the side of a hill and the border gate popped into view. Timon's heart leapt. He had forgotten what lay ahead — so mystified by the Bear's behavior.

"What *now,* Mrs. Hummingbird?" he said in a hissing whisper. "How do we shed this — appendage?"

Mrs. Hummingbird smiled winningly at Mr. Spang and said in a swift undertone, "We do not."

Timon stopped dead and stared as the large couple continued toward the border without a backward glance. The Bear was mad! No one would recognize Timon as either the Jester or the driver of the fake contagion wagon, and no one would suspect this wilting, shabbily dressed fellow on the mare was a king. It was the *Bear* whom the guards must not see!

No good trying to argue with him. That would only attract the guards' attention. And no doubt Mr. Spang would *bring* them by interfering at the top of his voice.

As he caught up to them he heard Mrs. Hummingbird saying in great distress, "They will not! Oh, they must not! Tell me, Mr. Spang, that they will not make me lift my veil!" She raised a black handkerchief to her face beneath the veil and sobbed. "I could not bear it! I could not — and must I watch as they paw through my bag? Paw through all I have in remembrance of the late Mr. Hummingbird? Oh, it is too much!"

Mr. Spang gazed at her with admiration. "What a fine woman!" he said. "What seemly modesty! What gracious, deep feeling!"

Mrs. Hummingbird made a small dismissing gesture and gave another sob.

"Fear nothing, my dear," Mr. Spang said. "These guards know who I am. They will not dare to inconvenience a friend of mine."

"Oh, Mr. Spang," the Bear purred. "I will be grateful forever. How shall I ever repay you?"

Mr. Spang's face brightened. "Perhaps on your return," he said, "you will — let me show you my village."

"I will be pleased —," the Bear replied, then broke off and gave Mr. Spang's hand an impulsive squeeze. They were next through the gate.

The baker leaned closer and patted the widow's arm reassuringly. "Watch how I have my way with them."

He and the guards greeted each other by name.

"This is my friend Mrs. Hummingbird," he said. "She is deeply grieved, you see, and I assured her you are men of feeling who will not wish to intrude upon a good lady's bereavement."

With a quick motion Mr. Spang slipped three gold pieces into the hand of the nearest soldier. He glanced back and reddened. The widow's cousin was watching. Mr. Spang scowled threateningly but got in return only a glittering smile and a wink. He resolved to separate the widow from her relative.

"You are quite right, Mr. Spang," the soldier said, bowing courteously to Mrs. Hummingbird after showing his closed hand to his friends. "Our condolences, Mrs. Hummingbird, and good journey to you. Very happy if we can make your way a little easier."

They opened the gate and Mrs. Hummingbird and Mr. Spang walked through.

"My cousins," the widow murmured, gesturing toward the others. The guards glanced at them briefly and nodded.

So, at last, they passed out of Zircon.

A short way from the gate, the road to Mr. Spang's village

turned directly west while that into the Green Hills continued north. Timon and the King stayed a discreet distance behind the couple to allow them their private farewells.

Timon stared back into Zircon.

"When we come back, King, it will be to face the Queen," he said, "and she will lift the curse." He laughed slightly, surprised at his own optimism.

"But will it be in time?" the King said, perplexing Timon.

"For what?"

"Have you forgotten the betrothal? She said she will never marry anyone else and yet who can know what —" The King shook his head wearily and pulled his hat lower over his face.

Suddenly Timon heard Mr. Spang's excited voice. "You must grant me the one favor, Mrs. Hummingbird — to hold me until we meet again."

"Mr. Spang, you know —"

"You cannot refuse me — surely! One glimpse — I beg of you!"

The Bear drew back. "Please, Mr. Spang — you promised you understood my feelings!"

But Mr. Spang was overcome by his passion. His hand darted out and lifted the veil.

"*A bear!*" he shrieked. "*A bear!*"

Chapter Ten

The Bear sprang.

Mr. Spang clutched at the black skirts and hung on. "Soldiers! Soldiers! A bear!"

Unfortunately for the Bear, the mourning dress was of fine quality stuff not easily torn. He struck at Mr. Spang but the man ducked. Timon ran up and brought him down with two hard kicks to the back of the knees. Instinctively Mr. Spang grabbed for Timon. The Bear fled toward the rocks. Soldiers pursued, hurling spears and shooting arrows.

Just as Timon jumped on the horse he heard a tremendous roar of pain and voices crying, "He's hit!"

Scarcely knowing what he did, he raced the horse up the road before the soldiers' attention could turn to them. They went up a small side trail and behind a pile of rocks. Only a short way into the Green Hills but the air was burning. He dismounted, wiped his sleeve across his forehead and leaned against the rock.

They waited in silence and finally concluded they had not been followed.

"Made himself a trifle too irresistible," Timon said in a flat voice. But his thoughts were different, full of self-reproach. Why had he not driven the Bear across the border? It was the *Bear* who had needed his help, not the King.

They headed in the direction Timon thought most promising to find the Bear, picking their way along a trail so narrow, so barely discernible that he thought it must have been made by some animal. Never intended for humans at all. They saw nothing of the Bear.

As the sun sank early behind the hills they found a small cave. Shelter from the wind and a small fire was all they had. No food and no covers, no water.

"Folly to search for him this way," Timon said as they huddled over the fire. "We wouldn't last another day. Tomorrow we find Jarvis."

"Will they remember we were with the Bear?" King Rolf asked as they came within sight of the border crossing the next morning.

Timon shook his head. "The guard will have changed." He stared across into Zircon and with a deep sigh pressed his heels against the mare's sides and flicked the reins. She shied violently, nearly throwing the King off.

"Not only you," Timon said, holding her in, stroking her neck. "Nobody wants to go back."

Slowly she calmed and they went back into the Queen's kingdom as easily as they went in to supper at the castle.

The White Crane Inn was a popular resort and they had no trouble finding it. The landlord was not easily pried away from his prosperous patrons to answer questions of the dusty pair but finally he gestured toward the stairs and said with a disparaging laugh, "The door with the *poem!*"

The poem said:

Don't bother to knock.
I will not hear.
Be silent as rock
Or disappear.
Is that clear?

Timon knocked softly.

He was not surprised that no answer came. He knocked harder.

Go away!

Take a sleigh!

"Jarvis — open!" Timon called, rattling the latch. "It's Timon!"

"I know no Timon," came the quick reply.

"Think about it!" Timon said angrily.

After a moment he heard muttering and the rustle of paper. The bolt was thrown back and Jarvis emerged with a distracted look. He blinked. "I'm sorry. I was — somewhere else." He motioned them in and held the door open expectantly even after both were in. He peered up and down the hallway, then shut the door and locked it.

"The Bear?" he asked.

"That's why we've come," Timon said. "You must help us find him."

You must have some special flair,

Or how else could you lose a bear?

"We did not *lose* him," Timon snapped.

Jarvis listened to the tale with an air of perplexity and, when Timon finished, pressed his fingertips against his forehead. He walked into an alcove with windows on three sides, took up the sheet of paper at the top of the disorderly pile on the small table and read it, silently forming the words with his lips. Then he handed the paper to Timon.

"Have I known something without knowing it?" he asked.

The paper was covered with scribbles and jots, all crossed out except six lines at the bottom, which appeared to be the poem in its latest form.

> *The walls are red; now hot, now cold.*
> *The hard rocks break and shake and fold,*
> *Curst by the wind and drowned by sun.*
> *Go to the place that's sought by none.*
> > *Find it there —*
> > *Barbarian's lair.*

"The Green Hills!" Timon cried. He plucked the green hat — a new one already! — off its peg and thrust it into Jarvis's hands. "Come!"

But the poet only twisted the hat between his fingers and walked back to the alcove. "I suppose that is it. I could not understand why I was writing such a thing in such surroundings. Come —" He beckoned Timon into the alcove and waved his hand at the surroundings. They were directly over the stream, looking into thick green trees. Downstream, willow branches trailed in the water and wild flowers and grasses bent in the breeze. For an instant, vivid memories and longings leapt up in Timon, but as quickly, he pushed them aside.

"The Bear cannot wait."

An extremely pained look crossed Jarvis's face. "But I know nothing more than this."

"That is more than we know," Timon said urgently. "You cannot refuse! Something may — *come* to you as we travel."

Jarvis looked fondly about the room, then pulled his hat on with a jerk. "I have paid for two more weeks — he cannot put me out before then!"

They bought new horses, one for each, and supplies, and once again crossed the border. No intuition or insight presented itself to Jarvis, so they headed in the direction in which the Bear had run. They asked each person they met — hill dweller and traveler — for news of the Bear, but none had seen him, or even heard word of him. Nor did *Barbarian's lair* in the poem mean anything to them.

Soon Timon, who had been riding lead, held back. "Go first, Jarvis," he said. "Perhaps you will *unconsciously* lead us in the right direction."

The poet led in a continued line east, then abruptly struck north, looking as amazed as they did at the turning.

The red rocks radiated like the walls of an oven. Timon's clothes stuck to him and perspiration ran into his eyes even when they rode in the shade of towering rocks. Several times he had to drag himself forward to keep the nearly unconscious King from swaying out of the saddle. Jarvis slumped over, the wilted brim of his new hat nearly hiding his face. Timon wondered if he could even see where he led them.

Ceaselessly came the rumble and hiss of rockslides, sometimes distant, sometimes slithering down and crashing where they had just passed. If only Jarvis's intuition spoke now as accurately as it had described the Green Hills to him!

They settled under a sheltered ledge as the sun disappeared.

96

"Find it there/Barbarian's lair," Timon repeated. "I suppose that means the Bear is in the hands of the Turmaks. I have heard that they hate the Hills but plague the fringes to rob travelers. A wounded bear with a bag of riches would be a catch of some importance." He stabbed at the fire that seemed to put out no heat at all. "They are thick with Vos. They will give the Bear to him — dead, because that is less trouble — and get the reward."

The poet swallowed his dried fish.

Such good cheer!

Why persevere?

Timon's glance shot up angrily, a scathing remark at the tip of his tongue. Then he saw the poet's slight smile. He shrugged and laughed. "I like things to turn out better than I expect, not worse."

The next day his pessimism was still strong but began to lighten when it became clear that Jarvis was not wandering blindly but leading them somewhere. The sun was obscured by clouds and it seemed by comparison as if they were riding in a cool garden until the wind started up, blowing abrasive dust into their faces.

Suddenly Jarvis held up a hand and reined in.

Timon climbed down and went to Jarvis, who put a finger to his lips.

"Is this — *the Barbarian's lair?*" Timon whispered, his eyes darting across the surrounding rocks.

Jarvis shrugged. "Don't forget how vague my powers are. Perhaps all this means is that it is time to settle for the night."

Timon cast him a disgruntled look. "It cannot be only —"

He stopped suddenly.

Raucous laughter rose nearby and a voice shouted words he did not understand.

He signaled the others to be silent and stealthily approached the voiccs. Flattening himself against a rock, he peered around it. Five men sat at a fire over which hung a black pot issuing a noxious odor. They were big men, burnt dark as if they lived entirely outdoors. All wore green and yellow doublets, but that was their only resemblance to Queen's soldiers. He had heard that Turmaks wore stolen soldiers' doublets so that they could get closer to their victims without being suspected. The doublets, hanging open, showed soiled white blouses and wide belts of elaborately tooled leather. They wore coarse black skirts that came to the knees and tall soft boots. Soldiers' helmets lay on the ground alongside a pile of gold coin. A beefy fellow, with a purple scar running from his left eyebrow into his hairline, wore the Royal Crown of Holm at the back of his head. Another, smaller and even scruffier, held out his hand, admiring two large rings, rings Timon recognized.

"*Kan tumet,*" the man said. "*Kan tumet cle*" — which was clearly high praise.

The Bear's portmanteau was open and upside down on the ground.

Timon searched for some sign of the Bear. Except for the portmanteau he saw none. He circled noiselessly around the camp peering into the shadows for any shape that might be the Bear, bound, unconscious or — dead.

Satisfied at last that the Bear was not here, he climbed back to the others.

"Jarvis, your powers are whimsical. They have brought us to the Barbarian's lair — a Turmak camp — not to the Bear but to

his *bag*." He laughed silently with relief. The Bear was out there somewhere, but at least he was not dead here. "We will have to get it back."

The others gaped.

"*We* rob the Turmaks?" the King exclaimed.

"How many are there?" Jarvis asked apprehensively.

Timon raised five fingers and both gasped.

"Let them have the jewels," King Rolf said vehemently. "They are cold stones compared to our lives."

"The Bear himself said he does not need the treasure to free his father," Jarvis said.

"But you know things he does not and you told him to take three hundred thousand kliner to the Plain," Timon insisted. "If he *does* need the treasure, it will not be because of us that he does not have it."

He did not wait for them to see the truth of his argument. "Empty your purse, sire, and give it to me."

The King opened his mouth to protest but thought better of it and did as Timon asked. Timon stuffed the purse with stones, then attached it to his own belt, where it looked for all the world as if it were about to burst with its riches. He then took his sash of pockets out of a saddlebag, withdrew two small envelopes from it and handed the sash to the King. One of the envelopes he returned to the saddlebag and the other he slipped into a pocket in his breeches.

"What do we do?" asked Jarvis. Clearly, from his puzzled expression as he watched Timon's preparations, his intuition gave him no idea what Timon intended.

"If I don't come back in a reasonable time," Timon replied

with a sickly laugh, "come and pelt rocks at them." Then he shook his head. "Go back the way we came. Go to the Crystal Palace, King. The Queen will not harm you, though she may ask many questions. Nothing will be changed except that you must find another Fool." He spoke grimly but already his thoughts were with the Turmaks.

He sighed, gave the bulging purse a pat, untied his horse and went toward the Turmaks' fire.

He led the horse across small stones that clattered loudly and in a carrying whisper warned the animal to be quiet.

"Stop!" a voice shouted from behind a rock. This did not surprise Timon. He knew the Turmaks spoke at least enough of their victims' language to make their demands known.

He jumped and stared about wildly. "Mercy!" he cried. "Mercy on a poor traveler!"

Two Turmaks showed themselves, swords drawn and pointed at his middle. Timon heaved a great sigh of relief and gestured toward the slovenly doublets. "Thank heavens! Thank heaven for you, soldiers! Never was a sight more welcome!" He pulled out a handkerchief and mopped his brow. "I was afraid I had fallen among thieves." He smiled like a poor idiot much reassured, and patted his fat purse. He did not miss the look that passed between the Turmaks. "May a weary traveler share your fire, gentlemen?"

They led him hospitably to their camp. Timon saw immediately that all the jewels and gold had been whisked out of sight. He would have to search for them.

He saw too the quick and eager looks they all gave his purse, their sly smiles. They were of one mind without a word spoken between them. A chicken ripe for the plucking.

If only they did not attack and rob him before he could rob them.

One of the men was stirring the mess over the fire, which Timon now recognized as beans. He warmed his hands and sniffed the air. "You have been so kind that I hesitate to ask, thinking you might take my question as an insult," he said in ingratiating tones, "but you fine soldiers are not going to *eat* this, are you?"

They looked at him startled. Then several laughed and the others groaned and the one who had been stirring said, "This, or rocks."

Timon shook his head gravely. "A military man leads a hard life. But your hospitality has been so gracious, maybe I can help." He went to his saddlebags and came back with the small packet, which he opened and held under the cook's nose. "Treasures of the Far East," he said. "Ginger, cinnamon, saffron, pepper. Perhaps a touch of cloves — they will never disclose the whole secret, you know. My wife would not let me through the door if I returned without it."

The man shrugged and the others quickly urged the traveler to do what he would with their dinner. So Timon poured a small amount from the packet into the pot. As he stirred and the men watched the pot and commented in both languages on how the aroma was already improved, he reached his thumb and forefinger into the small pocket of his breeches and took out a pinch of the other powder.

"Here — taste," he said. He held the spoon toward the cook. As the man took a swallow the others intently watched his reaction and Timon dropped the second powder into the beans. In a few minutes he was serving them up.

He did not give himself any.

The scarred man looked up sharply. "You do not eat with us?" He gripped his spoon in a threatening fist. "Why?"

"I have no bowl, captain. Perhaps when one of you is done —"

The man threw a tin cup at Timon. "Eat!" he said. "Or tell why we eat first."

Timon served himself quickly. "No reason in the world, sir — as you see." He took the spoon being offered and sat far away from the fire. He said little but laughed uproariously whenever the Turmaks did. This pleased them, as if they thought he understood their language. All the while he spooned the beans into his shirt sleeve.

Gradually the Turmaks became groggy. They rubbed their eyes and slumped over, spilled their food, and were asleep before they touched the ground. Only the leader was able to rise on wobbly legs and lunge toward Timon with an enraged growl. Before he had taken two steps he fell on his face.

Timon peeled off his coat and then the shirt, wiped the mess from his arm and threw the shirt aside. Finally he went through their belongings and found the gold and jewels in the portmanteau under a saddle blanket.

In a few minutes he, the King and Jarvis were riding in the near-darkness — anywhere, and as fast as the horses would take them.

They didn't know how long they rode until the King moaned, "Enough! They cannot find us tonight. Stop, Fool!" So they stopped under a ledge. King Rolf fell asleep immediately, and Timon sat with his back against a rock.

"Go to sleep, Jarvis," he said, "and have an enlightening dream. We will need you tomorrow." He was determined to stay awake all night. The Turmaks would follow if they had to follow for years and they would tear him apart joint by joint, delighting in his pain. The moon gave a cold, white light. He shifted, pulled the coat tighter around him and started as some small animal skittered through the sparse underbrush.

Chapter Eleven

He was wakened by the grip of a small hand jostling his shoulder and a voice saying urgently, "They are coming, Fool! Wake up!"

His eyes flew open and stared into a pair of very clear violet-colored eyes. A woman with graying dark hair knotted on top of her head but blowing loose in wisps caught by the slight breeze. The sky was turning light.

"Who are you?" he stammered.

"April Flower," she said. "Come — there is no time. Wake the others."

But she went to them herself and shook each by the shoulder. The King thrashed at her. "Let me be, Fool!" he complained.

"If we do not hurry," the woman said, "the Bear will bite off the head of my friend Nol."

A cry filled Timon's throat and choked him.

King Rolf bolted upright and stared wildly about him. "Timon," he cried, "what —"

"He is alive?" Timon whispered.

"Much alive," she said drily.

"But his wounds —"

The clairvoyant's expression sobered. "His leg."

"The one that was crippled?"

She nodded. "That is why he must be so careful. Come — if we do not get back his temper will get the better of his reason and he will never walk again."

Her glance fell on Jarvis, who was staring with open admiration.

Your fame travels far,
Like the light of a star.

April Flower gave him a quizzical smile. "You exaggerate, Jarvis," she said.

Jarvis's eyes lit. "You even know *me!*" he exclaimed. "Did I not say that April Flower has great power?"

"We must go," she said with a slight smile. "The Turmaks' desire for revenge will always be greater than their fear of these hills — do not doubt that." She turned to Jarvis. "Will you come or return to the White Crane?"

He let out a delighted laugh. "It is a *privilege* to see you work," he said earnestly. "I think I will never again call myself clairvoyant."

"Why not?" she said. "We work with the powers given. You are one of us."

Jarvis would not dream of contradicting April Flower. He nodded happily. "If it were a matter of *learning,* I would dog your steps until you cast me out. But it is not — I know that. So, now that this — adventure is in your hands, I'll make my way back."

She drew him a map, they mounted, and Jarvis, turning his horse west, said, "*Farewell, farewell, strangely-met friends.*

May you have joy and all that —"

His brow wrinkled and he broke into a chagrined smile. *"And all that best wends."* Then he laughed. "Come to see me if you are ever in Tippet. And bring the Bear. He will want to hear my new epic about bears."

He touched his hat and disappeared around a turn.

"Clairvoyant," King Rolf said as she started forward, "tell me Princess Jessy will not become betrothed to Zeltoun."

"I cannot, sire."

The King paled.

"I do not *know*," she amended.

"How — how is that possible?" the King asked, drawing her soft laugh.

"My powers differ from the poet's only in degree. I am not shown everything."

The King murmured inaudible disappointment and slouched even lower in the saddle.

April Flower led them north. Obviously they were not going along the main paths. The only people they met greeted April Flower by name and looked as much at home as she did. Finally the sun disappeared, but still they rode. The King was near collapse and complaining bitterly. Timon was nearly falling off his horse. But the woman held herself loosely and erect and seemed almost a part of her animal. Finally she looked over her shoulder. "We stop soon."

"Is it your place?" Timon asked. His throat was dry as sunbaked mud and his tongue stuck to the roof of his mouth.

She gave a quick laugh but no answer.

It was a small shack sheltered from the wind. There was nothing in it but a crude fire pit in the middle of the earthen floor and a pile of wood against the wall. While Timon built the fire and the King sat in one corner April Flower emptied the basket she had carried behind her saddle. Smoked salmon, bread, wine, strawberries.

Timon stared at the spread but could find no appetite, though a few minutes ago he had been ready to pounce upon it.

"Do you — *sense* anything more about the Bear?" he asked. "Is he all right? This Nol — he can quiet him?"

"Nol will impress on the Bear the fact that a cripple will not free his father. He will also remind him of the convenience and joys of walking and running and dancing." She saw Timon's face pale. "I feel he is all right for the moment."

He took the salmon she offered.

"Have I seen you before?" he asked, taking a bone from his mouth. "All day I have thought you are familiar."

She laughed. "When we met my appearance was considerably grander."

Timon's eyes narrowed. At last he said with elation, "When the Queen came. You were with her." To take such joy from remembering such a simple thing! Once his memory had been flawless.

"I am flattered you remember," April Flower said. "So much else happened that day."

Timon gave a short laugh. "In sooth!"

He took wine and watched her eat — elegantly, though she ate with her fingers. There were other questions to put to her but not in the King's presence.

Before long King Rolf had satisfied his usual small appetite and curled in a blanket beside the fire.

As soon as he knew the King was asleep he leaned toward April Flower. "Do you know the note that Princess Jessy wrote?"

She smiled into her wine cup. "I wrote that."

"But —"

"I saw what was happening between them. I knew the King would be more impressed with words from the Princess than from me."

Timon glanced at the King. "He will be disappointed. The note written by her own hand has been precious to him because they saw each other so briefly." He looked back at the clairvoyant. "This bear says he is not *the* Dancing Bear —"

"He is not."

"But he is a dancing bear — is there not some way he may *do?*"

Even before he finished she shook her head. "Never." She sipped and regarded him from lowered eyelids. "You are a strange one, Fool. You know what the note says — *she will try to kill him* — and yet you would take him to her?"

"*No!* I would tell him and we would find some safe way — after he has gone to his father."

Her glance flicked up to his. "You did not tell him when you made your bargain?"

"I think you know we did not. The situation was — different."

A small smile curved her lips. "What is he like, then — this bear of whom you are so fond?"

"I have not said that," Timon replied after a pause.

"So you are not fond of him?"

"You have been in courts, madam. You know that Fools are not fond — or unfond."

He found her smiling again, a kindly, amused smile. "Am I wrong, then? You see, I have taken you for his friend — that is why I have waited to consult with you before telling him anything more about his father."

"Consult with *me?*"

She closed her hand on his wrist and leaned forward. "His father is the Dancing Bear. *The* Dancing Bear. He is the prisoner of the Plains Turmaks and unless he is freed soon they will kill him."

Timon stared. He drew a deep breath and let it out in a thin stream.

"I'm glad you didn't tell him," he said finally.

"You think I did right? It was difficult — he roared that it was his right to know, and that is hard to deny."

"What good to *anyone* if he had rushed out — as he would have done — and collapsed before even reaching his father?" Timon took another deep breath. "The Dancing Bear is his father! Then if he is freed he can go to the Queen and the curse will be lifted!"

"He *may* accomplish that," the clairvoyant said. "It is not a certainty."

Timon turned on her. "But the note —"

"*The Dancing Bear* may *lift the curse,*" she recited.

"You were telling us a *perhaps?*" Timon cried. "A *might?*"

"Time was short and I am no grammarian. It has not been shown me if he will accomplish it or not."

Timon gazed at her in astonishment, remembering all the times he had gone to the parapet looking for the bear who would save them.

A small mocking laugh bubbled out of him. "You should have written more *ifs* and *maybes,* clairvoyant. Of course in our desperation we took the most comforting meaning." He made a dismissing gesture. "But that is irrelevant now. *This* is the bear who might lift the curse. You are certain he is the one?"

"Of course."

Timon raised his eyebrows at her but nodded. "Good. Then we must see he has the opportunity."

He reached into the shadows and brought out the Bear's portmanteau. He turned it over. Jewels and gold spilled onto the dirt floor.

"This is not worth three hundred thousand kliner," he said. "Why was he to take it? A bribe?"

She nodded. "A Turmak named Aard offers to help him escape for three hundred thousand kliner. Of course it is only cruelty — how can the bear get even two kliner? But he knows Aard could be bribed. The possibility and the impossibility enrage him. His turbulent thoughts are powerful — no wonder even the poet received messages."

"Perhaps this Aard will take whatever is offered." Timon stuffed the treasure back into the bag. "And why will they kill him when he is so useful?"

"Because Vos wishes it. Ibaz, their leader, resists strongly but he does not like to go against Vos."

"Vos!" Timon exclaimed bitterly. "As ever! — let there be evil and there is Vos. What is his part?"

"He does business on the Plain, much with the Turmaks. You know he will do anything to prevent the curse being lifted — so the King cannot have Princess Jessy. He guesses you and the

King will try to free the Dancing Bear and since he cannot find you —" She shrugged. "A dead bear lifts no curses."

Timon stared at her without expression. Then he said, "You know where the Turmaks are?"

She nodded. "Good," he said. "I will take the jewels and gold and —" Words failed as he pictured an entire *tribe* of barbarians like the ones he had already met. He swallowed and changed the subject. "And if the Dancing Bear is freed? Has he some magic that might lift the curse?"

"No magic. He must make the Queen forgive him."

Timon stared.

"Explain his departure," April Flower continued, "by claiming — temporary madness. The loss of memory. Some —"

"*This* is what our fate rests on?" Timon cried. "He must *talk* this shrewd Queen into believing some — *excuse?*"

"He must try," April Flower said. "Only the Dancing Bear can drive out the hate that infects her and only then will she lift the curse."

"Dreamer!" Timon mocked. "She will laugh in his face and have his head cut off. Tell this to some idiot — not to me."

Silence hung heavy between them.

"You cannot believe, so let him die?" April Flower said.

Timon turned on her. "I did not say that." He stared into the fire, then looked back at the clairvoyant. "Tell me where the Turmaks are. I will see what is — possible."

"The Dancing Bear is in a strong cage and well guarded," she said, "and you do not know which of them is Aard. There will be no second chance. Do you have a plan?"

Timon laughed. "A plan? What is that?"

Chapter Twelve

The light was only beginning to come when he woke, but April Flower was already about. Soon they were mounted, and soon the last of the cool was gone and the typical Green Hills day was upon them. April Flower was no more talkative than she had been the day before. King Rolf hung on and looked as if he were trying to keep himself in a state of semiconsciousness to block out his misery. Clearly he had heard none of April Flower's incredible story.

The sun was low when they rode through a particularly narrow cleft between vertical walls and April Flower stopped.

"Look," she said, pointing ahead.

"Your place?" He followed her gesture and blinked. Directly below and ahead were still the barren red rocks but beyond and all the way to the horizon spread a dark green plain that turned gold as it caught snatches of sunlight.

"The Plain of Waving Grass," April Flower said.

"It can't be," Timon said. "Everyone told me there was no way through the Green Hills that did not take at least four days."

"Incidental travelers do not know all the trails," she said with amusement, "and hill people never tell everything to strangers."

None of the fragrant cool that rose from the grasses carried into the Green Hills, but memory and imagination brought it up to Timon and he felt the urge to dig his heels into the horse's sides and ride helter-skelter into the beautiful green, to throw himself head-first into the dark gentle undulating waves.

"Who would guess the ugliness there?" he said. He flicked the reins and followed her. They had not gone far, between hills and piles of rocks but always returning to a view of the green plain, when she stopped again and pointed toward a plume of smoke that rose ahead of them.

"From my chimney," she said.

Around two turns and the house was before them. Seeing it, Timon knew why she had laughed when he asked if the shack were hers. This was large, of stone, with a wide veranda. Its windows were set deep and glowed now with yellow light.

Timon jumped off and ran to the door, nearly colliding with a small man with mustaches.

He grasped the man's shoulders. "His leg?"

"Better inquire of *my* health than his," the man said.

Timon laughed, thrusting the man aside, and entered. As he blinked, adjusting to the light, a familiar voice roared, "Is that the clairvoyant? I want to see you!"

The dimly lit room was uncommonly large and crowded. He threaded his way toward the door the voice had come through, sidestepping baskets overflowing scarves and trinkets, piles of rugs, trunks bulging with clothes. How would the Bear greet him? Except for the few words in Mr. Spang's company they had not spoken since he left the Bear stranded in the wagon.

He pushed the door open slowly.

The Bear was in a large canopied bed, propped against a mound of pillows. He was staring at the doorway scowling.

Timon smiled slightly. Found no words.

"Timon!" the Bear cried. "Timon!" He jerked forward. A spasm contorted his face and he reached for his leg. The pain passed and he saw Timon's alarm. "A twinge," he said. "Very dramatic. So they did not get you! I might have known. Or did you *talk* your way out?"

Timon's eyes widened. Then he laughed loudly. "What do you mean? Am I not known throughout several kingdoms as Timon the Silent?"

"Ah, yes — I had quite forgotten." The Bear beckoned. "Come in. How did you get here? Did the clairvoyant find you too? And the King? The woman would tell me nothing! And then she disappeared while I was asleep and left only that fellow who entertains me with stories of what my future will be if I move from this confounded bed."

"She brought us," Timon said. His smile faded. "Bear — I am sorry. This is my doing. I should have —"

"Fool, don't *bore* me," the Bear said. "I simply made myself too alluring to Mr. Spang. Did you hear him? — *One glimpse — I beg of you!* I believe he would have married me."

They were still repeating choice bits of Mr. Spang's conversation and roaring with laughter when April Flower and the King came in. Immediately the Bear sobered. "You, clairvoyant — enough of this artful dancing! You have things to say to me and I want to hear them!" His glance fell on the King then and softened. "Glad to see you, King."

"And you, Bear," the King said. He hoisted the portmanteau onto the bed. "I believe you dropped this."

The Bear stared at it. "How —"

"Later," Timon interrupted. "I'm starving." He went out and onto the balcony that overlooked the moonlit plain. He turned at the sound of footsteps.

"You looked at the leg?" he asked April Flower.

She nodded. "My experience is limited but I think it is mending. Slowly."

"I saw the pain it gave him. A twinge, he said. He musn't know how his father is threatened. Tell him everything but that. I will drug him so he cannot try to follow me."

April Flower nodded. "A bold plan so far. And the Turmaks?"

"I will need gaudy clothes, including a cloak or coat with valuable trinkets hidden in the lining." He waved a hand to take in her rooms. "I've no doubt you can provide. What *is* all this? Are you the Merchant Queen of the Green Hills?"

She laughed. "People come for information. Should they propose? Marry? Buy dates or sell dates? Plant a tree at the front or at the back of a property? And I get everything from pomegranates to clothes fit for the Queen herself. Will gold spoons in a cloak do?"

"Splendid. And we must polish the Royal Jewels. Where is the King? He is strangely quiet."

Nol joined them. "The Bear insists, April Flower. His roaring has already weakened your foundations — perhaps you should come."

April Flower nodded and looked at Timon. "You will not come?"

Timon shook his head. "He would read my face. If he asks, say I fell asleep."

He gazed across the Plain and brooded about facing the Turmaks.

April Flower came out after a few minutes. "He wants to see you," she said. "And then he wants to eat."

When Timon went in, the Bear motioned toward the portmanteau. "I claimed I did not need it," he said, "but that was stupid talk. How do I know *what* I will need? Thank you."

Timon shrugged. "The Turmaks wore the jewels so badly, you know — I couldn't let them keep them. I believe they would have stirred their wretched beans with the scepter."

The Bear gave him a long look. "Before long my father will be free. We'll all go to the Queen and she will lift the curse."

"That is certainly the plan," Timon said, concealing his own pessimism.

"She told me where to find the Turmaks," the Bear went on, "but I must wait a few days. No help to anyone if the leg doesn't work."

"Admirable sense."

"But I swear, not *many* days!"

Timon smiled slightly. "Why, surely no one expects *many* days of patience from you, Bear. Now let me tell them to bring food for me too."

In the kitchen he emptied a packet of tasteless, odorless yellow powder into the Bear's stew.

The Bear noticed nothing strange.

"She says it was the Turmaks who abandoned me," he said. "A crippled cub was no use to them — couldn't even be sold." He looked up. "Do you think she's right? Does she pick his thoughts out of the air the way she says?" When no reply came he said, "You're quiet. I hope you aren't turning sober."

Timon managed a smile. "This is not sobriety — it's fear," he said. "I must confess something which will not please you."

"Oh, that —" the Bear said, waving his spoon. "I already know."

"You know?"

"That you left something out when you recited the words of the Princess's note: the Queen loves him *and will try to kill him.*"

Timon gasped. "How could you know?"

The Bear motioned toward the portmanteau. "You didn't look inside?"

Timon shook his head. The Bear rummaged in it and came up with a folded paper which he held toward Timon. Even before he took it Timon guessed what it was.

"Where did you get it?"

"In a trunk in King Rolf's broom closet. I was suspicious of you and I always like to know what I'm getting into, so after you were asleep — you snore atrociously, did you know? — I went through the castle."

Timon remembered the sounds that had roused him that night. "I heard noises — I thought you were moving furniture."

"Looking in the trunks and hampers in my own room first."

"I don't believe it! You entered the King's bedchamber? And searched it while he slept in it? And mine?"

The Bear chortled then he grimaced and again stroked his leg. "And the First, Second and Third Chamberlains' bedchambers," he continued. "And the bailiff's and the silver pantry and the closet full of ledgers. Incredible amount of junk they've let accumulate."

Timon stared at him then began to laugh. "And the locks! — you picked the locks! You pick locks too!"

His laugh suddenly broke off and he stared at the Bear.

"You knew, yet you agreed to go to the Queen."

"I wanted the jewels."

He emptied the bowl and complained of being sleepy. Soon he drifted off in the middle of a sentence.

Timon prepared to leave.

"Perhaps the jewels will only be stolen from me with nothing gained," Timon said to the King. "I have your permission to take them?" He was separating the jewels from the coins, returning the jewels to the bag and leaving the coins on the table.

"Do not even ask," King Rolf said. "You will manage — you always do. You know I wish you well."

In the small hours of the morning he was told the shortest way to reach the Plain and given instructions where to find the Turmaks.

"Keep watch on the King," he said to April Flower. "It is an easy thing to underestimate him — his determination. Even his strength." He glanced at the door of the room where the Bear slept. "Three days' peace the drug should give you. Perhaps when we return he will be so happy to see his father he will forget to throttle me."

Once onto the Plain he dismounted and opened the portmanteau. When he was done adorning himself in all the Royal Jewels and back on the horse, he looked like a star moving through the grass, too brilliant, too dazzling to look upon.

He muttered how heavy it all was, took up the small lute that was tied behind the saddle and began to play and sing a troubadour's song as gaily as if the world were only flowers and sunshine.

Chapter Thirteen

It was nearly dusk when a flamboyantly dressed minstrel rode brazenly toward the Turmak camp singing a song of mild disrespect to an old hero. There was a rush in the nearby bushes. Shouts split the air — *"Ti ma! Stop!"* — and the next instant four long blades danced on Timon's chest.

"By all means!" Timon agreed, gentling his nervous horse. "Observe how totally I stop."

The four men were dressed in the white blouses, black skirts, and soft boots the other Turmaks had worn, but all were considerably cleaner. They wore jewelry around their necks, in their ears, on their wrists, embroidered into their vests. Timon saw that all the glittering stones were paste. The sight cheered him; perhaps they were so unfamiliar with real stones they would not know them when they saw them.

"Who are you?" barked the leader. "Why are you here?"

Timon tipped his crown and smiled companionably, hoping they were all extremely steady-handed. He did not wish to be run through by accident. "Timon of Furnal — troubadour and actor — at your service. I also tumble and juggle. I have heard there is no troupe finer than the Plains Turmaks and I hoped you might need someone of my incomparable talents. Let me see Ibaz."

They eyed his gaudy ornaments with exactly the same eagerness of the other Turmaks when they had looked at his pebble-stuffed purse. He was not surprised when the leader knocked his spear against the crown and said, "You waste our time, clown. Leave this and the rest and go."

At these words Timon began to laugh, which annoyed the Turmaks.

Another came close. "What is funny?" he barked, prodding Timon's chest with his spear. "Let me run him through, Held!"

Held waved him away. "Take off the jewels," he ordered.

This only set the minstrel laughing again until Held gave him a sharp stab. "You'll think it funny too," Timon said, sobering slightly and rubbing his chest. He touched the chain and the crown. "Fakes. Very good — you agree? I had them made specially."

"*Makan!* Lies!" they all shouted.

Timon shrugged so unconcernedly that the leader put out his hand. "I will see."

So Timon gave him the crown. Held peered at it, turning it in his hands, holding it to the fading light. "You look," he said, handing it to the man next to him. This man was even less certain and said so. They grouped and talked in loud undertones and finally surrounded Timon again.

"Come with us."

"Exactly my idea," Timon said. He had not understood their discussion but knew why they took him: they were afraid to make a decision and would leave it to others. That way there was no danger of either letting a fortune pass through their hands or returning to their camp with a collection of imitations.

As they approached the camp men, women, and children crowded around. They skirted a huge fire in the middle of the encampment and stopped in front of an elaborate tent where a huge black-bearded man sat. He was dressed like the others except that the embellishment of his clothes was more sumptuous, with heavy bands of silver and gold thread. Two men, each in a loose-fitting robe also encrusted with embroidery, stood behind him.

The black-bearded man motioned to Held. "What is this?"

"Ibaz, he says he is an actor and the jewels are not real."

"Give me the jewels and search him," Ibaz commanded.

As the jewels were taken and the cape torn from Timon's shoulders and dropped to the ground he protested, "I understood the Plains Turmaks are not robbers like their Zircon cousins."

They laughed uproariously at this and finally Ibaz said, "But if someone attacks our camp — as you do — and we capture him, it is fair we punish him, no?"

Once again a round of laughter until Ibaz motioned for the men to get on. Hard, practiced hands searched him, untied his sash and began to empty its pockets onto the ground.

"Stop!" Timon cried, grabbing for it.

Ibaz raised his hand. "Ah! — we find something! Let me see."

As he thrust his fingers into the pockets Timon went toward him. "Medicines, spices, dyes — nothing else." Ibaz stuck his nose into one pocket and sniffed.

"Coriander," he grunted.

"And fennel and sage," Timon said. "Nothing you do not have yourself."

Ibaz inspected each pocket, feeling carefully as if he might find a pearl in the powders and crushed leaves, then tossed the sash back to his prisoner with a nod and motioned his men to continue the search. They pulled off his boots and felt into the toes. They shattered the lute to be sure nothing was attached inside. As if by an afterthought, Held picked up the cape and began to feel through it. He let out a whoop, ripped the lining, and began to pull out gold spoons. Another and another until there was a pile of twenty-four beautiful spoons glistening in the dust.

"Clever," Ibaz said without rancor, "but not clever enough. We are masters at this. We miss nothing. And these —" He motioned toward the Royal Jewels that lay at his feet.

"I appeal to your sympathy, sire," Timon interrupted. "Let me keep my precious jewels. I admit to you my talent is not extraordinary. It is these —" he laid a hand to the crown "— that farmers and coarse villagers come to see.

"A duke once offered three hundred thousand kliner for these — yes," Timon said, "you hear me right. Three hundred thousand. A fair bargain, I thought." He winked at Ibaz, who let out a crack of laughter. "But before I could collect the three hundred thousand the duke's appraiser came. Curse the man! I was undone, of course. The duke nearly exploded. He was so angry that he let loose his bear to chase me out of his territory."

Ibaz threw back his head and let go a shattering laugh. "*Menghin pa'an!*" he said. "Scoundrel!" — not without a touch of admiration. "Try such a trick on me and I will tear off your head!"

Timon smiled and shrugged, making Ibaz laugh again. As he sobered he said, "You are a bad actor —"

"You are cruel, sir," Timon said in an injured tone. "I only admitted I am not superb." Ibaz chuckled. "But you cannot blame me for trying — who would not like to be part of your company? Let me perform. Judge then and you may be surprised."

Ibaz regarded Timon, drawing his hand down his beard. "Yes!" he shouted suddenly. "Stay. Tonight you perform — we will see." The man behind him whispered in his ear. Ibaz nodded. "Tomorrow," he amended. "Other business now."

Timon bowed. "As you say."

"And keep your toys." Ibaz motioned toward the glittering pile. "Nobody who hides gold spoons so carefully will wear real jewels in the open."

Timon was escorted to one of the other tents and shown to a straw-filled mattress in the corner. He lay back to await the visit of Aard, pushing from his mind the possibility the man had not taken up the broad hints of three hundred thousand kliner and a bear let loose, or that he might not even have been in the group that was listening.

It was dark and he had finished a meal of fiery-spiced meats and ale so strong it nearly tore out his throat, before his visitor came.

The tent flap was raised. One of the men who had been standing behind Ibaz entered. His eyes flew quickly about the shadowy tent and, when he was sure they were alone, he came quickly to Timon. A long, high-bridged nose and pointed chin, thin lips topped by a straggling mustache that hung below his jawline.

"I am Aard," he said, peering to see if his name had meaning for the minstrel.

Timon sat up and crossed his legs. "You are ready to sell the bear?"

The man drew in a sharp breath. "How do you know? No one has heard me say it."

"Except the bear," Timon said.

Aard's eyes narrowed. "How —"

"Will you sell the bear or not?"

"Beware how you talk to me, clown. I have power here."

"Do not waste my time, Aard." Timon gestured impatiently into Aard's glare. "Have we any business?"

"You have brought three hundred thousand kliner?" the Turmak asked with a sneer. "You have nothing Ibaz does not know about."

"I have the Royal Jewels of Holm," Timon said, motioning toward the jewels piled beside him.

The man stared at them and let out a sharp laugh. "Fox!" He picked up the scepter, holding it like a club and turning it near a candle. Then he took up the crown and each piece in turn. In the flickering light Aard's eyes gleamed and he made delighted, savoring noises. But when he had examined the last piece he turned to Timon in anger.

"Two hundred thousand at most. I said three hundred thousand."

"And everything the woman April Flower has — you know her?" He could tell by Aard's reaction that he did. "Then you know she is wealthy."

But even before he stopped, Aard was waving his hand in a quick negative gesture that ended with his pointing toward Ibaz's tent. "There is no time. Vos knows others are looking for the Fighting Bear. He says to kill it now."

"Vos is here *now?*"

Aard nodded.

"Then we must work quickly," Timon said. "Two hundred thousand is not three hundred thousand but where will you get more? Help me get the bear out and it is yours." He gestured toward the pile.

Aard stared at it for a long moment, stroking one side and then the other of his thin mustache. Suddenly he said, "Tomorrow night I open the cage. Give me the jewels."

Timon gave a sharp, insulting laugh. "When the cage is open you get them."

Aard cast him a malevolent glance and stalked out.

As he waited for the others to fall asleep he searched for some plan to get the Dancing Bear away immediately. Only an idiot would rely on Aard. More safely rely on him for a knife in the back.

He had thought of nothing when he finally stole out. He did not even know where to look for the bear. There was no sound but the occasional stamping and snuffling of horses and all the tents but Ibaz's were dark. Finally he crossed to the far side, where he saw the glow of torches and heard murmuring voices. He approached cautiously, listening and peering into the dark, and saw the bear.

He was huge. Gaunt. His eyes sunken. Fur coarse and grizzled.

Suddenly he batted at an insect and cast an immense sweeping shadow snatching at the night. Timon blinked. Any Queen could love such a creature. No wonder Ibaz resisted killing him, even for Vos.

The bear moved to the back of the wheeled cage that was lit by torches, and turned his great back on Timon.

Two guards were throwing dice nearby. Timon took a deep breath and approached them, sauntering in a careless manner, raising a hand unconcernedly when both jumped and pointed spears at him.

"So this is the famous Fighting Bear," he said.

"Who are you?"

"Just an unemployed minstrel — guest of your leader." The one who had not spoken whispered to the other and the weapons were lowered. "I would like to see the bear closer. You do not mind?"

As Timon approached the cage he felt the Dancing Bear's eyes on him. He did not move so Timon went around near him. "I come from — your son," he said in an undertone.

The Dancing Bear stiffened. A long moment passed before he whispered, staring at the guards instead of at Timon, "My — son?"

"He has come far to help you," Timon said gently. "It is a long story and —"

The bear's paw shot out and lifted Timon by the throat. "What is this?" he hissed. "Some elaborate prank of Aard's? You will be sorry —"

The noise disrupted the guards, who peered toward the cage. They decided the minstrel had been teasing the bear and had angered him. They laughed and lost interest.

"No! No!" Timon said, choking. "Let me talk — you're killing me."

"No — if I wanted to kill you you would be dead," the Dancing Bear said, thrusting Timon into the dust. Timon brushed himself off and went back toward the bear but stayed outside his reach.

"He scarcely limps now," he whispered. "And I come from April Flower."

The Dancing Bear's face clouded with bewilderment, as if he heard words out of a very distant, barely remembered past. When he spoke he whispered again, "My son?"

"A fine dancing bear like yourself," Timon said, going nearer. But the bear was not listening. He had turned from Timon and was staring into the black. After a while he said without looking back, "What is this long story?"

Timon told him everything he knew of what had happened since the Dancing Bear left the Queen. The bear did not move, and Timon did not even know if he was listening. When he was done the silence between them was very long.

Finally the Dancing Bear said, "He will be all right?"

"If he will let the wound heal."

The bear nodded, then finally he came toward Timon. "It is not true I left the Queen that way. I overheard Vos talking with a confederate. They were planning to substitute paste for the Crown Jewels. I was so absorbed in what they said I was careless. His men came up on me." He paused a moment and then said, "In short, they drugged me and when I woke I was in the hands of these people. I learned Vos had wanted to kill me but his Turmak friends persuaded him to take money for me. He cannot resist treasure."

Timon stiffened. Vos! Not even the Queen, but Vos! Every evil thing that had happened to him, to the Bear, to the King, to the Dancing Bear, to April Flower, to all the bears that had been killed and banished — every evil thing sprang from *Vos!*

"He is here," he said in a voice he could scarcely control.

"He is often here," the Dancing Bear said drily. "What do you mean to do now?"

"Kill him," Timon said through his teeth. Then he heard his words. He closed his eyes and shook his head. "No. It is only what I would like to do. I must get you out but I don't know how."

In silence they thought vainly for a solution.

Finally the Dancing Bear said, "You took a great risk coming alone. April Flower says I can persuade Princess Alys — *Queen* Alys —" He smiled slightly. "Perhaps she will always be Princess to me. April Flower says I can persuade her to lift the curse?"

"She is uncertain, but sure that no one else will."

"And that is why you took the risk to free me?"

"Of course," Timon said curtly.

"No," the Dancing Bear said much to Timon's surprise. "I hear it in your voice. You do not believe I can do it."

Timon gave him a slight apologetic smile. "No insult, sir. It is only that I recognize an — unpromising situation when I see one."

"You have come for another reason," the bear said. "I hope he is worthy of your friendship."

Timon stared.

Then he laughed. "Ill-tempered," he said, "and an accomplished lock-picker." He gestured toward the elaborate lock that hung from the cage door. "Would he were here now."

They lapsed into silence until the seed of an idea began to sprout in Timon's mind and he muttered under his breath, "A *third* time?"

"Three may be lucky," the Dancing Bear said. Timon started.

Did he too read minds? He turned a wary eye on the bear. But no, he only had very good hearing. He was smiling in a faintly mocking way. Having his joke even now. How like his son.

"We will see," Timon said. Without another word he grimly felt around his waist and went back to the guards. He gestured toward the small keg nearby. "You do not mind if I have some?"

They only grunted but made no objection when he took one of the tin cups hanging beside the keg and began filling it. They nodded appreciation when he refilled each of their cups, and paid no attention as he squatted to watch their game. However, when he took a pinch of powder from his sash and dropped it into his cup without offering to do the same for them, they glared expectantly.

"What is that?"

"Mountain clove," Timon said. "Just a hint of mountain clove. It is a peculiar taste of mine."

"Give us some," they demanded, shoving their cups at him.

"You will not like it," Timon warned. "It is bitter." And indeed the powder to put them asleep most quickly was very bitter, too bitter to have put into the beans.

"Give it to us or we take it," the tall one demanded. "*Hata!*" So, grasping full well the meaning of *hata,* Timon hurried. He dropped powder into their cups, which they stirred up with their fingers. They sipped and were scarcely able to screw up their faces and curse the bitterness before they fell over unconscious.

Timon snatched the key that hung from one guard's belt and ran to the cage. He fumbled a second with the complicated lock and finally threw the door open. The Dancing Bear stared at the unobstructed doorway but quickly recovered and rushed through it.

The instant his paw touched ground wild commotion broke loose. Screams. Shrieks. Running feet and clanking weapons, and above the melee, Ibaz's voice shouting, "The bear! *Hata!* Stop them! *Ch'in hata! Ch'in hata!*" as though he had looked across the camp, right through the tents, and seen the bear escaping.

"Go to the Green Hills," Timon whispered urgently. "Her friends will take you to her. Tell the King I could not save the jewels."

The Dancing Bear hesitated but Turmaks rushed toward them, their fierce shouting like the roar of wild animals, worse because the words were foreign. Their weapons and jewelry clanked and glistened. Their eyes and teeth were white lights in the dark.

"It's better we separate," Timon said. With a quick nod the Dancing Bear ran into the dark. Timon darted in the opposite direction. He crashed through shrubbery that scratched his face and arms, stumbled over stones, and finally dove into a thicket, where he huddled close to the ground scarcely breathing.

The wild Turmaks thundered past, setting the ground trembling, kicking dust and clods into his face, deafening him with their incoherent cries. At last they passed and when he was certain no more were coming he crawled out, so shaken they might as well have stampeded right over him. He moaned and had no more than raised himself onto his knees when strong cold fingers closed around the back of his neck and a silky voice whispered into his ear, "Surely, Fool, you are not leaving without greeting us."

"Ah, Vos," Timon said after a long moment, "how it pleases me to see you."

Chapter Fourteen

"Make a fool of Ibaz! *Ang chung darkhan!*" Ibaz screamed, his face bent so close that Timon could feel the heavy hot breath. "*Jatai chat!*"

Vos laughed and leaned toward Timon, who had been tied wrist and ankle and thrown against the center pole of Ibaz's luxurious tent. With an insidious smile he said, "Hair of the worm's belly. Roach's tail. You see, I understand the essentials of their language."

Ibaz grasped Timon's collar and shook him until his teeth rattled and his eyes bulged. "No man makes a fool of Ibaz! You will see — *Din chahar fu jen! Anyang gelug salar!*"

"Breath of the wild boar," Vos translated. "Slime in the eye of the dead fish." As Ibaz continued his colorful tirade in two languages with punctuation in blows and kicks, Vos turned his gaze fixedly to the Royal Jewels of Holm that were piled in a basket beside him. Then he said, "Enough, Ibaz — I cannot stay all night."

Ibaz broke off an epithet and turned to Vos. "We will make him tell where are this April Flower and the others you seek," he said with fervor. He did not like failure. Most of all he did not like it in front of Vos and so far this day there had been much failure in front of Vos, beginning when Vos recognized the jester

133

he was looking for from Ibaz's description of the amusing minstrel who had wandered into the camp. Now he was anxious to
erase the stain. "Give him to us, Vos. We can make him talk."

But Vos shook his head and smiled unpleasantly at Timon.
"That is my pleasure now." He barked out a name and when one
of his retainers entered said, "We leave now. Put the Fool on a
horse."

And so Timon was trussed up on a small mare. Vos took the
leather bag which Ibaz surrendered reluctantly and attached it to
the back of his saddle. The Royal Jewels of Holm, no doubt. Vos
mounted the stallion and Ibaz, still much disgruntled, said, "We
will find the bear and kill it."

Vos was strangely uninterested. "The Fool will lead me to
him." He leaned toward Ibaz. "The merchant is more important.
I would not care for a blunder in that direction."

Ibaz looked up, his eyes like two slits of black light. "We have
never failed you there, Vos."

"Then see you do not begin now." Vos motioned to his men,
who rode heavily armed, three pairs ahead and three behind. It
appeared Timon was to have the honor of riding beside Vos
himself.

He was considerably startled when, after they had ridden only
a few minutes, Vos said in a conversational tone, "You will not
find more skilled assassins and spies than Ibaz's people. Their
extra talent lies in always being able to arrange that some poor
innocent is blamed. They have had all my custom for many
years."

Timon gulped. "All your killing and spying?"

Vos laughed. "Of a certain kind. Right now they are engaged
to eliminate the wine merchant of a Plain town who does business

in Zircon. He not only refuses to pay my — er —" He sneered. "The tax that I lay, but encourages others to defy me. However, Ibaz's services are expensive. Some troubles can be managed by less costly means. Simple enough to bend the law and pronounce a man guilty or plant goods in his residence and accuse him of evading the tax on such goods." He chuckled, a soft, savoring laugh that sent cold up Timon's spine.

"I can see how such enterprises would amuse a man of your imagination," Timon said slowly. "How tedious to merely uphold and enforce the law."

"Exactly!" Vos cried with a shout of laughter. Timon glanced at him sharply. He had much experience of Vos — too much. He had heard his laugh many times and he had heard many things in Vos's laugh. Malice, ridicule, scorn, brutality. But never before mere enjoyment. "I knew it! You must believe me when I say that the only thing I have regretted about this curse over Holm is that you are part of it. Such a waste! Now, if you had come to me instead, we might have done very well together. You cannot know how hard it is to do a great many things, and to have a great many things, and never be able to talk with anyone about them." He looked at Timon with an appreciative eye. "It was your idea, of course, to travel in the sham contagion wagon — a genius stroke!"

"I cannot imagine why I admit this, Vos, but in fact it was the Bear's idea."

Vos studied him for a moment, as if indeed he could not imagine why Timon would tell the truth so unnecessarily. Then he said, "Yes — we concluded the bear at the border had traveled with you. Who is this bear?"

"You must ask him if you ever meet," Timon said, mustering

an even voice though he did not expect Vos to accept such eva-
sion calmly. His captor's head jerked up and his mouth tightened.
Then he laughed softly. "You will answer all questions in good
time. Why spoil our ride with unpleasantness?"

But Timon's thoughts had wandered. He was imagining the
meeting of the two bears.

"Is there something in your situation to make you smile?" Vos
said impatiently.

Timon looked at him. "I was savoring being called *slime in the
eye of the dead fish.* I must remember those. How many Fools
have the use of such endearments?"

Vos laughed. "Ibaz is a refined fellow. Let me teach you his
niceties."

After a short language lesson Timon said, "You seem to have
little interest in his finding the Dancing Bear."

"Bah! His people will not go into the Green Hills. No —" He
paused and looked shrewdly at Timon. "Even *I,* who go through
the wretched Hills so often, am not such a fool as to wander off
the main road. I will not even squander my men by sending them
without knowing where to go. If I choose to, I can even wait until
your friends come out to try to see the Queen." He laughed.
"You are surprised that I know they will do this? It is their only
move. They must tell her the true story of why the Dancing Bear
went away. She will soften, they think. She will be repentant and
lenient. Except toward Vos, who has deceived and cheated her
for a very long time." He spoke the last words with unmistakable
pride and humor. "Well," he continued, smiling at Timon, "you
see why I must stop such a plan.

"Yet your friends may be overly optimistic. It is not at all clear to me that the Queen will be so pliable merely because the Dancing Bear returns and tells the story of the grievous wrong done him." Once more Vos interrupted himself with a self-satisfied chuckle. "Her hate is very deep — as I should know since I have nurtured it so carefully. It may be she will believe me as against the Dancing Bear. But I will not allow it to come to that.

"As for the King, perhaps I should kill him outright instead of waiting for the curse to do him in. The Princess would be unhappy, but that would pass. One day she would turn to me."

Timon glanced sideways, comparing his pale, evil-visaged companion with the King. Even in the King's cursed condition the comparison was ludicrous. Vos was optimistic indeed! "But she is to be betrothed to Zeltoun. Were we misinformed?"

"She is not only betrothed but marries him almost immediately."

"Then —"

The stallion snickered just then, raised its head and sidled, but was quickly brought under by Vos. "You see," Vos said, "even my horse laughs at that. Surely, Fool, you do not endow Zeltoun with *immortality*. He may die. He may even die rather soon. One does not know."

"Ibaz?"

Vos gave an elaborate shrug and laughed, and then launched into a chronicle of his extensive and profitable association with the barbarian Turmaks. He continued without pause into the night, and it became clear to Timon that there would be no stopping for rest. He lapsed nearly into unconsciousness. He heard the drone of Vos's voice but marked the words only in disjointed phrases, and ceased making a pretense of listening. He was too tired to care whether he was whipped into attention or allowed to sleep.

Vos did not wake him. The indulgence was a surprise but Timon had no illusion why Vos was amiable with him.

Vos's nature was so untrusting, and his secrets so rank, that he must always keep his affairs and innermost thoughts to himself. He could get no praise for clevernesses, for tricks shrewdly maneuvered, for achievement attained by daring if bloody deeds. How it must gnaw at him, a vain man, that his brilliance must go unappreciated. Until now, when he came into possession, as it were, of someone whose intelligence and wit he did not despise. Now he could pour out the whole history of his genius; it was safe to talk because Timon would not live to tell the secrets he heard.

Some time later he woke. Vos seemed to be asleep even though he sat as straight as ever. Timon pulled and tugged at the ropes that bound his wrists in front of him, but the knots were secure. Ahead none of Vos's men gave any indication of being asleep. None even slouched in his saddle or nodded. When he twisted to look at the men behind, the two nearest met his eyes instantly. Nothing sleepy about them. By then they were in the Green Hills, sheltered from the wind at the moment because they rode between vertical walls. A turn could bring them full-face against a gale or a dust storm. He looked to the tops of the cliffs. Were April Flower's friends watching? He saw nothing but the jagged outlines of the rock against the moonlit sky.

Then he fell asleep, and wakened in the scorching sun, his body dripping perspiration, his head throbbing even though it was shaded from the direct sun by the sunshade that had been attached to his saddle.

He was right about Vos.

The man talked all the way through the Green Hills. He talked even when the heat turned his skin a peculiar lavender tinge. His speech slowed and several times he glanced into the sun as if he would murder it. Once when he caught Timon's eyes on him he hissed, "Something to stare at?" It was the reaction of a vain man seen at less than his best. Timon shrugged and looked away.

Vos paused in the narrative of his brilliance only to receive Timon's sometimes admiring, sometimes wry, sometimes acid comments on his larceny, graft, corruption, and general treachery. It seemed to Timon prudent to keep his captor in good humor. He would never extract mercy from Vos — as well hope for laughter out of roots — but as long as he was alive there was no telling what opportunity might be thrown his way. At the same time, even if he could have managed it — which he doubted — Timon didn't think cringing servility would please Vos. On the contrary, Vos seemed delighted with insults. He had laughed uproariously when Timon remarked, "It would be a great pleasure to be in your service, Vos, if only you were a totally different person."

They ate sparingly from baskets packed by the Turmaks, the same fiery stuff. "Their taste is not subtle. Wait until you see my table," Vos said. He spoke boastfully but distractedly because he was listening to the rockslides. Timon knew by then that though Vos went through the Hills often, he feared and hated them.

They slept in the saddle again. And the next night. And another.

Finally they topped a rise and Zircon spread away from them green and rolling, with trees and shade and the river. The sight was almost as welcome to Timon as the Plain of Waving Grass had been. Earlier he had hoped for something to slow their progress through the Hills. He did not expect to be rescued; April Flower had many friends but they were not trained fighters as Vos's men were. He had simply wanted some sign that April Flower knew where he was. Now, however, he had given up that hope and wished only to be out of the Hills.

As soon as they entered the Queen's land Timon became aware of a peculiar excitement taking hold of Vos. Often Timon found a stare fixed on himself, as if Vos knew some deep and hilarious secret. Several times he laughed aloud, blowing out the laugh as if he could not hold in his mirth. Finally, when they were heading east he leaned toward Timon. "We are going to my residence," he said. "I have something to show you." The smile on the pale face was so smug, so satisfied, it was ghastly. Timon managed a slight one in return and said, "I hope it is the splendor of your dungeons."

Vos's mouth dropped open and he stared dumbfounded. Then he began to quake with laughter. He leaned over the stallion's neck and let out wave after wave of delighted guffaws, shouts, snickers.

When he finally seemed calm Timon said drily, "That is not the best line I have ever got off, but it is certainly the best response."

Once more Vos was set off. Even his imperturbable guards looked around surreptitiously. "You will see why," he said. "You will see."

Vos's residence was an uninteresting stone structure of medium size. One would have guessed that its owner was a man of modest fortune and austere tastes.

They passed between guards who looked every bit as wooden

and formidable as the ones who had come through the Green Hills, into a hall furnished with pieces that were elegant but old-fashioned and worn.

"Most of these are cast-offs from the Queen. One cannot quarrel with the original quality," Vos said.

"And are your dungeons furnished with cast-offs from the Queen's dungeons?"

Instantly he wished he had kept silent, for Vos flew off into maniacal laughter again. He was bent over gasping when he seized Timon's arm and said, "I cannot wait. Come!"

He grabbed up the bag that held the Royal Jewels and with the other hand propelled his prisoner through a heavy oak door and down stone steps lit by candles set into niches in the wall. Timon noticed that no guards came with them.

"I am going to show you my dungeons," Vos said in an excited whisper.

At the bottom of the steps was a cellar. It was small, the size of a common storeroom, but circular and absolutely empty. When Vos took the candle from the niche near the foot of the steps, Timon saw that there were no cells, no evidence of any prisoner having been held in the place. Nothing but wood shorings and walls of crudely cut stone block.

Vos handed him the candle and said, "Please do not disappoint me by trying to make mischief. You would never get past my men." He took from around his neck a narrow cord of black leather, at the end of which hung a small key. He took the candle and approached a section of the wall. His back to Timon for an instant, he applied the key to the lock. Or so Timon supposed; he had seen nothing in the wall that resembled a lock.

There was a harsh grinding sound, a whir, and a section of the wall swung open. Vos stepped into the dark and held the candle high.

Timon's mouth fell open. His eyes strained in their sockets, and observing this Vos laughed with delight.

"My humble dungeon," he said. "My own humble dungeon."

He entered and flitted about touching the candle to other candles and lamps so that the glimmering that had stunned Timon when lit merely by the one candle, gradually became a cavern of brilliant glancing lights and lustrous surfaces.

Vos disappeared. He had gone into another room or behind some obstruction but to Timon it seemed as if he had been consumed by a bursting light. He reappeared, his candle out. He waved a hand to include the whole chamber.

"Come in! A unique dungeon, don't you think?" An intense gleam in his eye and a high, giggling laugh. He closed the door.

Timon swallowed. He stared at casks spilling jeweled necklaces and bracelets, girdle chains, brooches, buckles, and clasps, at a harp of gold with a sounding box in the shape of an eagle with eyes and claws of emeralds, at plates, bowls, and goblets of purest gold. Candles were held in sticks and candelabra of silver and gold encrusted with jewels. The lamps were of gold filigree with pendants of stones that cast reflections against the ceiling and walls. The carpet was of the costliest wool, colored by the rarest dyes. There were statuettes and armor, weapons, wine vessels, mirrors with jeweled frames. The walls were hung with tapestries and the furniture was carved and gilt and inlaid with ivory and precious stones. A book lying open near Timon was written in gold letters upon vellum tinted purple. Others were bound between plates of gold.

"This is carrying frugality too far," Timon said, to the utter delight of his host.

Vos opened a chest and took out a garment of peacock green silk embroidered in imitation of butterfly wings, which he slipped over his black tunic. He straightened it with caressing fingers and stood before a mirror caressing his own image with his eyes.

Then he took his prisoner on a tour of his treasure house, picking up one piece and another, holding each to the light, and then thrusting it upon Timon to admire.

He pointed to the brocaded bags that crowded the carved shelves against one wall. "Perhaps you think they are stuffed with gold coin," he said. "But it is only nuggets." Whereupon he emptied three bags of gold lumps onto the carpet. Three other bags, these of gilt leather, rained unset precious stones. He dragged his feet through the nuggets and jewels as if he could feel them with his toes, and led Timon toward the far side of the room, behind a carved screen, into a smaller chamber lined with shelves. Upon these shelves were stacks of gold coin and in the middle of the carpet was a pile as high as Timon's knees of more coin.

"I am still counting, you see," Vos said. "I am *always* still counting, the stuff pours in so fast."

He waited for Timon to say something, and when he did not, turned on him. When he saw his prisoner's face his pale eyes narrowed. "You look upon this and are tired?" he barked.

"It is the curse," Timon said. "I would be tired if my head were inside a lion's mouth." Without asking Vos's leave he returned to the other room and lay down on the nearest couch, upon a cover of gold cloth so fine that the pattern of the brocaded cloth beneath it shone through.

Vos glowered down at him, purpling with his gathering rage. It did not please him that the only person who had ever been admitted to his treasure house should fall asleep after merely glancing at the hoard and making ironic remarks. "Fool!" he shouted, jerking the gold cloth from under the offender.

Timon sat up.

"Enjoy this while you may," Vos said through his teeth. "When I return all will not be so exquisite." He took off the silk garment. He was all in black again, the cruelty and mocking in his face — the familiar Vos was back.

"When I return you will take me to the clairvoyant." He raised a palm. "Don't bother to tell me you cannot find her. I know better. We would go now except that the Queen demands my presence at the wedding. Do not waste your time devising ways to escape, because there is no escape. My men do not know how to get in; they do not even know where the door is."

He preened before the mirror. "I have been companionable," he said. "Perhaps I have even liked you, but expect no favors for *that* — I would rather kill the Dancing Bear, and anyone else who threatens me, than *like* someone. There will be nothing companionable about me if you are uncooperative when I return."

He went to the door, inserted the key into another keyhole Timon had not seen, and went out. The door closed with the same whirring and a resounding thunk.

Chapter Fifteen

Timon stared at the door. He was stunned and dead tired and — what he would never have imagined he could be — sick of the sight of riches. He closed his eyes, then raised his palms against them; it seemed to him his eyelids could not keep out the glare of Vos's hoard. In the blackness of his closed eyes he thought of the wedding and wondered if the King knew it would be so soon. What would he do when the Princess was married? What joy in listening to stories about a Princess who was married to someone else?

He went into the room with its neat stacks of coins and pulled down all the carefully counted stuff. A childish gesture but worth something to him. If only he could turn the gold to lead.

He lay on the couch and, without being aware he did it, slept.

He woke considerably refreshed and wondered immediately what time it was. There was no way of knowing. He imagined the pale miser among his riches, his eyes and his fingers feasting, his wretched laugh leaping out. What use to him to know the time of day?

He took up a branch of candles and went to the door. After much searching he found a tiny keyhole behind a movable shard of mirror that made up part of the elaborate frieze around the doorway. He stuck the pin of a brooch into the keyhole and jerked it about but was not surprised when nothing happened. He next examined the hinged side of the door but could not even find hinges. He knew the door was of stone on the outside. On the inside it was iron, so he did not bother trying to batter it down.

He carelessly pulled tapestries down and knocked shelves to the floor to examine the walls of the rooms. He found no crack or chink, nothing that could be another exit.

There would be no escape until Vos returned.

He snuffed all the lamps and candles except a single branch, and lay down again.

He dozed and woke, dozed again.

He was wakened by a scratching sound from the direction of the door. Impossible — surely Vos could not be returning already. Though how could he know that? — he had no idea how long Vos had been gone.

He tiptoed to the door and put his ear to the lock. Definitely something scratching at the lock. He picked up the Royal Scepter of Holm, raised it over his head and pressed close to the side of the door, scarcely daring to hope that it would swing open.

The jerky scratching continued for what seemed interminable minutes. Suddenly there was the click and the whir. Timon drew in a deep breath. He gripped the scepter so hard his arms trembled.

The door swung open and a dark form entered cautiously. Timon swung desperately, striking the intruder across the back of the head. A fierce cry went up and Timon was grasped around the waist by two immense hands and the life nearly squeezed out of him.

As suddenly the grip was loosened and he was lifted up and staring into two blazing black eyes.

"Of course!" the Bear shouted. "Go to considerable bother to find a Fool and he'll strike you dead for your trouble!"

Timon gaped at the towering figure. Then he gathered his wits and shouted back, "Humbug! You scarcely felt it and you nearly cut me in two!"

"I wonder why I didn't — after that fine stew you served." The Bear came in and looked about. He reached into one of the trunks and came up with a pawful of jewelry that sparkled in the dim light. He held it closer to his eyes and said, "Are you all right?"

"I'll do," Timon answered, still breathless with surprise, relief, and aching. "You?"

The great figure moved farther into the shadows with only a slight limp, shrugging as it went. "Well enough."

"Shouldn't we get out of here?" Timon said. "How did you get past the guards?"

"I sent them all on a long vacation." He let a pawful of coins chink to the carpet.

Timon carried the branch of candles toward him. "And the Dancing Bear? Did he —"

"Very impressed with your daring and originality."

"Is he your father?"

It was a while before the Bear answered, coming back into the main chamber. "It appears he is. Odd having a father after — *not* having a father." He stopped and stared at Timon. "Thank you."

This time it was Timon who shrugged. He put the candles on a table and began stowing the Royal Jewels in the leather bag. "The King?"

"Ah — the King," the Bear said after a pause that could only be ominous. Timon turned quickly. "He was gone when April Flower and Nol woke after seeing you off. Needless to say, he was off to see the Princess. April Flower asked her friends to look for him but there was no word when I left." He added quickly, "But her friends are everywhere in the Hills. I'm sure he's taken care of."

Timon digested this news with alarm and then said thoughtfully, "He must have known your father would come first with us. I wonder if he was making plans all the time he was so silent."

"It appears you were right," the Bear said, peering at a silk hanging composed of millions of tiny knots. "Obviously this journey has been good for him. What a surprising fellow!"

The Bear turned from the hanging, cast a look of disgust about him, and said in an altered voice, "We have an appointment. Let's get out of this foul place."

In a few minutes they had invaded Vos's kitchens. As the Bear said, the guards were unconscious, strewn about just as they had been dropped.

Timon tore the leg from a partridge. There was no need to ask how the Bear had opened the door in the cellar; he had proven before how expert a lockpicker he was. "But how did you find the door?" he asked. "I'm sure his men know about the cellar but he said none of them knew where the door was. I couldn't see any trace of the door or the lock."

"One of them told me about the cellar letting onto a secret room. Poor blackguard was scared out of his wits." The Bear popped an entire meat pie into his mouth, pushing in the few stray crumbs with delicate flicks of his claws. "After that there was no problem. I found you and the door by your smell."

"By my smell!" Timon's voice trembled with outrage. "My *smell!* Of all the —"

The Bear stared at him with some perplexity and then let out a roar of laughter. "*Your* smell — *Vos's* smell. Your *human* smell, Fool! There is a prodigious human smell around the area of the door, where the rest of the wall smells only of rock."

But Timon had been too shattered to laugh. "Fortunate for you you *danced* and did not *talk* for your living," he said.

The Bear only smiled and pushed three cherry tarts into his mouth.

They took a small supply from Vos's stores, found horses. The Bear glanced into the sky. The moon shone now, dodging in and out of dark clouds. "Hurry!" he said, swinging onto the horse. "It is later than I realized. They will not wait long."

Timon mounted. "What is the *plan?*" he asked. "What are we going to do?" But the Bear did not reply, only galloped in the direction of the Crystal Palace without waiting to see how closely Timon followed.

The road was deserted. Sometimes they went between hedges, sometimes through stands of slender trees, sometimes across open field. It was turning light when they clattered down a shallow bank, across a small stream and on the other side left the road and entered a grove of dark trees. The Bear put his paws to his mouth and made an owl's cry. In a moment it was returned. "They are still here," he said.

No sooner had he spoken and dismounted than they were greeted by the Dancing Bear, who came out and, saying nothing, took Timon's hand between his great forepaws. Neither did he speak to his son, exchanging only a long glance and slow smile with him. Behind him came a woman dressed in a splendid court gown of heavy silk and lace. Her hair was glistening gold.

Timon stared. "Who —"

"It is good to see you, Fool. Do you like my yellow hair?" the woman said.

"April Flower!" Timon blurted as the Bear said, "What is this?"

April Flower laughed loudly and threw something at Timon which he caught in midair but did not look at as he said, "The King —"

She shook her head soberly. "There was no word when we left. But my friends are everywhere. They will care for him. No doubt he is back at my place by now."

But Timon had been through the Green Hills twice. Both times he had gone through as easily as anyone could — he had no doubt of that — and both times there had been moments he doubted he would survive. How could the King survive alone? April Flower said her friends were everywhere, but that was obviously a gross exaggeration and he could take no comfort from it. What had he said to the Bear? Ah yes — *he must make the journey if only for the bracing discomfort.*

Bracing discomfort! He let out a mocking laugh, and then his depressing thoughts were interrupted by April Flower's tugging at the cloth over his arm. "Put it on," she said. "And the rest."

He held it up and saw it was a doublet.

"Our disguise," she said. "We go to the wedding as the Countess Marilla of Ruvin and party. You have heard of her, Fool — the renowned eccentric so proud few affairs are grand enough for her. A distant cousin of the Queen, in fact — so there is no doubt she received an invitation. We bear her coat of arms — thanks to my memory and art. And this —" she touched her wig "— gives me enough resemblance to her that we will be admitted without question. Very few even know what the Countess looks like."

"And if she comes?" the Bear asked.

"Her own daughter married a Prince and she would not go to the wedding. She certainly will not stir when a distant cousin marries a man who must wait for his father's death to become merely Baron."

The Bear laughed. "Very good," he said. "The guards, the ministers, even Vos himself will be so awed by the Countess's presence they will tumble over themselves to please her."

Timon turned to him. "You did not know? I asked a dozen times what the plan was and you never said you didn't know."

The Bear let out a short laugh. "I *never* say I don't know."

"How could he know?" April Flower said. "Once my friends told us Vos had you we could not keep him long enough to make any plan — only shout to him as he ran out that we would wait here for the two of you."

When Timon looked around again at the Bear he was no longer there but had gone to examine a fine cart with a coat of arms painted on its sides and back. In it were two large chests, elaborately carved and painted in gilt and red with huge hinges and latches of polished brass.

"Each about the size of a bear," the Bear observed when the others came up.

"They will search," Timon said. "Everything that crosses the bridge is searched."

"Not today," April Flower said. "Of course Vos will want to search, but the Queen will have none of it. *She* would never submit to search if she went to another castle. She would turn around and leave. And she knows her guests would do the same. Vos must swallow his suspicions for once."

And Timon, with his experience of court life, knew she was right.

Before long the Countess Marilla's party was on the road. The Countess rode a splendid roan and was followed by the wagon, driven by a diminutive fellow wearing livery of red and orange, the colors of the Countess's house for hundreds of years.

The road was nearly deserted, coming as it did from an isolated area and not merging for some distance with the main thoroughfare that led to the Dark Lake.

They had been going a few hours, attracting the admiration of peasants who swept them bows and curtseys and children who ran alongside until they were exhausted, when a ragged man who had been walking wearily ahead turned as they came nearer and ran into the road.

"Stop!" he cried, frightening the horses with his wildly waving arms. "Stop! You must let me ride with you!" He was red with sunburn and covered with dust. His hair stood out in all directions and several days' growth of beard stood on his chin. "Where are you going? I must have a ride!"

April Flower was about to ride around him when she suddenly reined in and cried, "King Rolf! Is it you, King?"

The man looked at her with starting eyes and gasped. "What?"

Timon leapt from the cart and ran forward. The King backed from them cautiously, as if ready to dart away even though he seemed too tired even to walk. "You are mistaken," he said. "I am no king. Do I look like a king?"

"King —," Timon cried. "Don't you know me?" He tore off the orange cap and red wig, the bushy false eyebrows. King Rolf squinted at him.

"Timon!" he whispered. "Is it you?" He ran to Timon and embraced him. "I'm so glad you're safe!"

"*Me* safe, Majesty!" Timon exclaimed. "You have come through the Green Hills alone."

The King laughed softly. "Well — not alone. April Flower's friends found me wandering — very hopelessly, I fear. Once they were persuaded I would not return to her place they told me the best way to continue. Another and another helped." He smiled as he shook his head and wiped a sleeve across his perspiring forehead. "No — I did not come through alone." He turned suddenly. "April Flower! Is it? But what is this? Are you going to a masquerade?" Before they could reply a desperate look came into his eyes. "I have no time — She is being married today! The man said the Princess consented because the Queen threatened *me*." He motioned down the road. "This is the way to the palace, isn't it? How far is it? I must —" He paused to catch his breath. "I must have one of your horses," he said. "You can ride with Timon, April Flower." He glanced at the sun and said, as if to himself, "How much time do I have?"

"King," Timon said, "do you not recognize a grand party on its way to a royal wedding? We are all going together."

With great perplexity King Rolf looked from Timon to April Flower and back again and seemed speechless.

"Of course we all go together," April Flower said.

"Oh," the King said finally. There was still bewilderment in his voice, as if he had been solitary so long and was so convinced he must rescue the Princess by himself, that he had difficulty accepting the idea of not going alone. Then with an abashed smile he said, "Well, good! Good!"

"He must get in with one of the bears," Timon said. "He is not dressed for the Countess's party."

"The bears?" King Rolf repeated. "Both? They are both safe? I am glad to hear it." His forehead wrinkled. "But what are they *in?*" Timon motioned toward the chests. The King looked and turned a shade paler. "I must get into —" He stopped, swallowed, and nodded. "If it must be."

"Unnecessary," April Flower said. She untied a bundle from the back of her saddle and threw it to the King. "Put them on. I thought we might meet you, King — all roads lead to the palace today."

As she spoke there was a creaking from the cart. The Bear lifted the lid of his chest slightly and said in a dry tone, "Welcome, King. Now may we get on with this?"

Chapter Sixteen

The main road to the palace was a stream of unsurpassed grandeur. Standards bobbing and snapping in the breeze. The sun glinting and shimmering off polished weapons. High-stepping, fine-bred horses in elaborate trappings, and carved and gilt coaches carrying men and women dressed in dazzling magnificence — headdresses of fantastic shapes, embellished with peacock feathers and floating plumes, capes and tabards of velvet edged with fur, flowing sleeves with brilliant linings, gold and jeweled girdles, and chains, necklaces, bracelets, brooches, and fillets of all the precious metals and stones. Horses carrying bags of fine-worked leather and brocades, bulging with anyone might guess what splendid gifts for the marriage couple.

As April Flower predicted, the wedding guests were not detained at the bridge. Servants hurried forward to unload the chests from the Countess's cart. Six men groaned under the weight of each, and if Vos had not been observing, they would probably have dropped them unceremoniously to the stone floor.

But Vos, in his accustomed black, like a raven among finches, watched with avid eyes as the chests were pushed and tugged to the place, near the door to a small chamber, where the Countess demanded they be set. It was unclear why she chose that spot but no one thought to question her. Even less did anyone think to contradict her wish.

After she had wandered away Vos said to the Countess's servant with the carroty hair and bushy eyebrows, "Only solid gold is that heavy. Do you know what it is?"

The servant stifled unseemly laughter and, with a reticence befitting his station, murmured, "I do know, sir."

"Do not mumble at me!" Vos barked. "What is it?"

"Incredible treasure, sir. Diamonds the size of fists, books with pages of gold, twelve goblets carved of pink jade — to name but a part."

The light leapt in Vos's eyes. "As I thought! As I thought! The Countess can well afford chests of incredible treasure." His eyes darted about. He pried at the locks and said in an undertone, "I will look. Open them."

"The Countess carries the keys, Minister."

Vos gave a low growl, then shrugged. "In good time, then," he murmured. "In good time." He wandered off among the milling guests and it seemed to Timon that he could scarcely keep his fingers from stealing out to tear the jewels from wherever he saw them.

As he watched the miser a blare of horns announced that the ceremony was about to begin. Vos ran up the stairs to join the procession. At the top he stopped and turned to survey the gathering of riches as if searching for some way to carry it all to his cellars. The guests, unaware of the Minister's designs upon their possessions, took seats at the cushioned benches facing the dais opposite the staircase.

As soon as Timon saw all attention focused on the groom and Prelate at the dais, he unlocked the chests, and the bears climbed out and slipped into the small chamber beside the staircase.

A band of lutes, harps, and muffled drums began to play the

music of the wedding procession. First down the staircase came girls in yellow scattering flower petals, then the Queen. She paused a moment to gaze smugly upon the magnificence she had assembled. Her eyes passed over the golden-haired woman who stood nearest to the bottom of the stairs, then darted back with recognition just as April Flower ran up, grasped her wrist and pulled her down the stairs. The Queen was so startled she could get out only a strangled cry before she was pushed into the small chamber and the door slammed shut.

Vos had been a few steps behind with the Princess, but when he saw what happened he cried, "Guard! Guard!" and ran down. He did not see how the red-haired servant, who had started up the stairs toward him, smiled and nodded as he rushed to the small chamber and pounded upon the door bellowing, "I am Vos! Open this door! Open! Let me in! I am Vos!"

The door flew open, Timon shoved Vos in and followed, shooting the bolt as he did so.

The Queen was stamping her feet, waving her fists and shouting at April Flower. "What is this, traitor? I will have your head! What is this?"

April Flower made a deep curtsey before her, which placated the Queen not at all, and motioned toward the far corner.

The Queen's glance followed and she gasped. "*You!*" she whispered, "*you!*" for she recognized the Dancing Bear, though he had changed much in fifteen years.

Vos had seen him too. He leapt toward the door but was tripped by the servant. As he picked himself up he saw the servant peeling off his false hair.

"You!" Vos said in a tight, croaking voice. "You — how?"

"Cut my way out with diamonds," Timon said.

The miser's eyes bulged. His face purpled and his fingers reached like claws for Timon's throat. He caught them back when the Queen turned to him. But she did not even see him. She was so astonished, so torn between the urge to embrace the Dancing Bear and the urge to set her guards on him, that she saw nothing.

Vos straightened himself and stared at the Queen a moment, then said in a voice betraying nothing of his fear, "You have waited a long time for this, Queen Alys. Who would have expected the false one to deliver himself into your hands? Nothing could be more suitable for this grand occasion."

The Queen turned slowly back to him. His was a voice familiar and trusted.

"You may have revenge now for the long days and nights you wept for him, Majesty," Vos continued. "I will get the guards."

The Queen had hurt and hated a long time. Not a day passed but she cursed the Dancing Bear. Vos's words, his very voice, reminded her and inflamed her rage. She raised her hand to give the order.

"Princess," the Dancing Bear said. The voice was so changed and yet he called her *Princess* in that tone she remembered as if from yesterday. She turned to him with a look of anguish. "Vos lies," the Dancing Bear said gently. "As he has always lied. I have not been false to you. I did not desert you." He told the story of his abduction and imprisonment in a few words, putting no emphasis on his own suffering. As he spoke tears started in the Queen's eyes and when he was done she went toward him with open arms.

"He was ever the good storyteller," Vos said smoothly, stopping her. "Have you forgot, Queen? Do not let him make a fool of you a second time."

"How would I dare to come now if I had been false to you? Why would I come?"

Vos gave a sarcastic laugh. "To do the very thing he appears to be doing, Queen — to play on your sorrow and win back your good graces. Now that he is old and life is hard without your protection he would like to install himself once more in his comfortable place. It is good reason to come. What is more simple than that?"

The Queen felt herself weakening.

No — Queen Alys of Zircon was not a fool twice.

She stiffened and strode toward the door, anxious to have the Dancing Bear removed from her sight.

"You do not believe him," the Dancing Bear said.

"Why not?" the Queen snapped, not daring to look at him. "He has served me well a long time."

"Majesty," April Flower interrupted, "the Dancing Bear says Vos was substituting paste for the Crown Jewels. Examine your crown."

Beside him Timon felt the spasm that shook Vos.

"You suggest for fifteen years I have worn paste without knowing?" the Queen said with scorn.

"Vos would use fine-quality paste and he has friends who know how to get such stones. I know you well, Queen — you take the Crown Jewels for granted. I have never seen you examine them."

The Queen stared at her indecisively.

Then the Bear, who had come around near Timon, said, "Why

do we waste this time talking? Take the crown off, Queen, and look at it."

She turned to him. She had not noticed him before but was not surprised by his presence.

She nodded slowly. Her ringed fingers reached up and took off the crown. She carried it toward the window, not seeing how Vos struggled to get loose from the hold the Bear had on him.

As she went near the Dancing Bear her eyes lifted to his and they stared at each other a moment. Then the Dancing Bear smiled slowly and the crown dropped from the Queen's hands. With a sob she threw herself against him.

A great sigh of relief traveled the room. Timon unbolted the door and they left the Queen and the Dancing Bear to their reunion.

"Where is the King?" Timon asked the Bear, who held Vos imprisoned in his grip until the Queen would tell them her pleasure.

"And the Princess," April Flower said.

"And what is happening here?" the Bear said, waving his free paw toward the crowd of wedding guests. It had not panicked or scattered. Not one person seemed curious about the disappearance of the Queen and the disruption of the ceremony. Instead everyone stood calmly facing the dais and no one spoke.

Then they noticed that someone *was* speaking. From the other side of the room, beyond the crowd, a deep, droning voice. Before they could identify it the crowd let out a joyful shout and pressed forward.

Timon and the others pushed through. Emerging finally at the dais they found King Rolf and Princess Jessy embracing and the Prelate holding his hands over them in a gesture of blessing.

"What is this, King?" Timon cried.

The King left off the embrace and looked at Timon and the others with a radiant face.

"Why," he said with a laugh, "we could not let the kind Prelate leave without performing his duties. We are wed!"

The Princess threw her arms about April Flower and left tears on her cheek. "It is true," she said. "Is it not magnificent?"

"But what of Zeltoun?" April Flower said.

The now-Queen of Holm laughed. "He would not listen to reason, so the King persuaded him — most forcefully." She pointed to the side of the dais where the would-have-been bridegroom sat grasping his stomach.

"My friends —" King Rolf gestured toward the smiling assemblage "— recognizing me, agreed the ceremony should continue — so here we are. Quite *bound*." He grasped his Queen's hand and laughed merrily.

Another cheer rose from the crowd, which then began to break up and head toward the lavish tables that had been laid in the Dining Hall. All were so delighted by the unexpected event to which they had been party, none noticed that Vos was struggling in the grip of a live bear.

By the time they departed one and all agreed this affair would never be surpassed. The surprise marriage, the reunion of the Queen and the Dancing Bear, the lifting of the curse on Holm, the discovery of a staggering hoard in the Minister's cellars, the banishment of that Minister and the curse placed on him: that he should wander alone forever in the Green Hills — could any tale be more romantic?

The Queen insisted this was the last curse she would ever lay but, knowing the Queen was still herself even if somewhat mellowed, everyone took her promise with caution and praised her good intentions.

Her nature was so sweetened that she even received the newlyweds with good grace after her clairvoyant pointed out how bountiful such an attitude would seem to her guests. April Flower also mentioned how small Holm was compared to Zircon and observed how large was the nearby kingdom of Quire — and how handsome its new King.

The Turmaks were routed and driven into the Green Hills by the Queen's loyal men. Those known to have been Vos's confederates in corruption were sentenced to hard labor. Their first task was to break up Vos's residence stone by stone after the lower chambers had been emptied.

April Flower moved back to the palace, and the Dancing Bear took up residence in a simple but exceedingly comfortable suite with the best view across the lake.

The Bear remained with his father, for they had many years to make up.

When the King received word the refurbishing of his castle was completed, his party prepared for the return to Holm.

"It is different from living on the road," Timon said to the Bear, indicating all the comfort with a wave of his hand. "For myself too — the King has given me a permanent place and choice chambers. He is planning great balls and festivals, and they say his cooks are quite recovered from the curse and have perfected dishes of succulence never dreamed."

The Bear nodded. "The Queen's kitchens are — extremely adequate." He popped a cake into his mouth. "It is interesting for a while." He looked about at the servants crossing the Great Hall and the laughing courtiers and ladies-in-waiting standing about. "But I am used to other things. I'll go to Merth eventually, as I planned, and maybe to the Eagle Lakes."

"They are beautiful," Timon murmured.

When he departed the next day the Bear was at the gate. He smiled lazily and waved his great paw.

It was reported some time later that, sure enough, he had gone to Merth.

The curse was obviously off.

Every day Timon felt his strength coming back. Unbidden he would break into elaborate spurts of tumbling and one-man pageants of song and story that were much praised.

Elegant crowds flocked to the court of Holm. There was entertainment of great beauty and wit, and certainly the cooks were nothing short of astounding. But from the start Timon was aware of a vague restlessness he had never felt before.

After a few weeks he told the King, "I think the time has come for me to move on, sire."

"So things go too well here," King Rolf said. "You must have new audiences to conquer?"

"Perhaps that is it," Timon replied without conviction.

"Where will you go?"

"I don't know. Have you any recommendation?"

King Rolf thought and then said, "Morler is on the river. A beautiful place. I spent two weeks there once — royal obligations, wouldn't you know? — and nearly died of boredom. Perhaps it's a challenge like that you need. I'm sure if I gave you a letter to the Duke —"

"Nearly died of boredom?" Timon repeated woodenly. The very phrase sent shudders through him.

But the more he thought about Morler, the more he thought the King might be right. Perhaps he needed the challenge of making a dull place into a live one. Finally he announced his decision to go there. From King Rolf he got a fine praising letter, assurance that he would always have a place in the Court of Holm, and a fat purse.

But even the prospect of such a formidable challenge did not dispell the small gnawing sadness he felt. He did not know what caused it or what might cure it.

He was not one for sentimental leavetakings and so was surprised to find himself stopping at the inn where he had first met the Bear.

The Inn was a changed place — as was every place in the kingdom. At tables set under the elm that had suddenly sprouted new branches and thick leaves, travelers and locals chattered as they ate and drank. The interior was almost unrecognizable since its windows had been cleaned and all the cobwebs and dust cleared away, the walls whitewashed and the floors scrubbed.

He took in all these changes unconsciously because as soon as he entered his eyes went to the far table where the Bear had first been.

He blinked and blinked again for there — *now* — sat the selfsame Bear, holding a mug of ale in midair and showing all his fine teeth in what was definitely a smile.

Timon hurried through the crowd.

"What are you doing here, Bear?"

The Bear wiped the back of his paw across his upper lip.

"Life at the Crystal Palace is pleasant but a trifle dull for one so used to the road," he said. "I thought it might be."

Timon nodded.

"But I understood you had gone to Merth."

The Bear nodded. "An overrated place. And they say the Eagle Lakes are too."

"Then where do you head now?" Timon asked, scarcely daring to hope the Bear might be persuaded.

"Toward the river, I thought. There are many towns along its bank I have never seen. We bears now go everywhere safely, you know. And the welcome is prodigious."

"I head for Morler," Timon said. "On the river. A fascinating place, I am told. All manner of amusements and never a dull moment."

The corner of the Bear's mouth twitched as he turned the cup and stared at the motion of the ale.

"Perhaps I will try Morler too," he said. "You make it so appealing." He emptied the mug. "What do you say to our traveling together that far?"

Timon's heart leapt and he felt the sadness going.

"I believe I could tolerate the company," he said.

They had been walking some time and had left the border a few miles behind when the Bear suddenly burst out laughing. Timon gave him an enquiring look and the Bear said, "No — I don't believe I will let you think you have tricked me again. The truth is, I heard you were leaving the King this morning and going to Morler. I also know what a truly fascinating place that town is."

Timon turned deep red. Then he realized this meant the Bear

166

had purposely waited for him at the inn and had hoped all along that they might go to Morler together.

He laughed. "You are wrong, Bear. Any town is fascinating when I am in it."

The Bear gave a great shout and with a swipe of his paw sent Timon sprawling in the cool grass beside the road.